the
VIDEO VICTIMS

BY ROBERT WALLACE

CHAPTER I

EMPTY HOUSE

The Phantom

It was not a pretty city through which the man in a light car was driving, making a brief inspection of the town before heading for his destination. Mill towns rarely are attractive, and the original buildings of this one, now falling in ruins, once had gone in for gaudiness. But soot from many tall smokestacks had faded their gilt to a drab gray.

Even the name of the city did nothing to add to its beauty. It was called Uncas, after one of its founders.

But it was an important city. Its markets catered to a wide rural population, besides two hundred thousand local inhabitants. It was bustling, up-to-date, and progressive.

The man who was looking it over from behind the wheel of his car was about thirty-five, a man so average in appearance that there was no single outstanding feature about him. And in his quiet, dark clothing he was not an individual to whom anybody would give particular notice.

But that mediocrity of appearance was not remarkable where this man was concerned, because it was distinctly manufactured. He was in disguise, yet there was no visible trace of the fact that in his rightful identity he didn't look like this at all.

It was an expert bit of work, but disguise was one of the assets to this man in his chosen profession, an art he had long and carefully studied.

He had reached such a peak of perfection that it was doubtful if any other expert in the art of makeup could achieve such results as he did. But then he was that legendary character so feared by the underworld that his very life often depended upon his ability to change his appearance quickly and efficiently — the Phantom Detective.

After making a tour of some of the city's main arteries, he finally pulled up before an imposing home in the exclusive residential section. It was an old-fashioned mansion of many rooms, with high ceilings, cupolas, and a porch around three sides of the house. The grounds surrounding it were fenced in, and neatly kept up. It looked like a good, solid, substantial and comfortable home. Beside the gate was a name plate which read:

CHESTER McLEAN

The Phantom got out of his car, glanced at his watch and saw that it was exactly nine-thirty. He was right on time for his appointment. Opening the gate, he headed along the path that led to the house. At times trees and shrubs cut off the faint starlight to such an extent that he had to slow up for fear of wandering off the path and into some of the flower beds which were dotted at intervals between the shrubbery.

Finally he reached the porch and rang the door bell. There seemed to be rather a long wait before the door was opened by a strikingly pretty girl. She was in her early twenties, tall and willowy, with brown hair, and eyes that were a startling green. The tailored suit she wore, obviously expensive, enhanced a figure which was all that could be desired. "Good evening," the Phantom said. "I have an appointment with Mr. Chester McLean for nine-thirty."

The girl smiled, and he liked the way her lips parted. "Oh, I'm sorry, but Dad isn't home yet. If he made an appointment with you, though, he'll surely be here soon. Please come in."

The Phantom followed her down a wide, imposing old-fashioned hall and into a huge living room. It was big enough to hold two grand pianos, back to back, without their seeming enormous. Above the fireplace was an oil portrait of a handsome man. His features, and those of this girl, resembled each other.

The Phantom sat down, thanked the girl for a magazine she handed him, and sat back to wait. She didn't ask any questions but went over to a small ornamental desk and busied herself there.

A telephone rang somewhere in the house. The girl hurriedly excused herself and went out to answer it. The Phantom heard her voice clearly at first, then a door clicked shut and the voice was cut off. He shrugged, and settled back with the magazine in which he became so immersed that not until he glanced at his watch did he suddenly realize that it was after ten o'clock. The girl had gone to answer that call more than twenty minutes ago.

The Phantom placed the magazine on a table beside his chair and studied the room, appreciating its comfort and quiet elegance. Chester McLean, apparently, not only liked beautiful things, but could afford them.

Gradually, then, the Phantom became aware that the big house seemed deathly still. There wasn't a sound to be heard, not even a creak. No low murmur of the girl's voice, muffled by the door. And it should have been heard in such silence.

The Phantom arose, frowning thoughtfully. Moving over to the door, he took a few steps into the hall, went down it to the door the girl apparently had closed when she began telephoning. Even here he couldn't detect a sound. The Phantom grasped the knob, turned it slowly, and opened the door a crack. He realized that he was probably being presumptuous, but he didn't like that ghastly silence.

The room was illuminated — and nobody was there. The phone was in its cradle. The Phantom walked across the room to a window. It looked out toward the three-car garage, which was brightly lighted and the doors of two of the stalls were wide open.

The girl, then, must have gone off. But that seemed odd. It was neither polite nor safe to leave a stranger in that house alone. The Phantom returned to the hall. He raised his voice in a shout.

"Miss McLean," he called. "Miss McLean!"

His voice came back to him, but no other sound. Finally, he reached under his coat and touched a heavy automatic in a shoulder sling, reassuring himself that it was in proper working condition for action. Determinedly then, he began a search of the big house, instinctively sure he would find something radically wrong.

Every room on the first floor was empty. On the second, he found that four of the six bedrooms seemed to be little used. One of the other two was obviously the girl's, and the other was her father's. A masculine room, faintly smelling of expensive pipe tobacco.

Now thoroughly aroused, the Phantom even inspected the vastness of the attic and, at the last, the garage. Finished with his thorough search, it was quite plain to him that he was entirely alone in this big house, and that even the grounds and out-buildings were deserted. Then he remembered that he had forgotten to look in the cellar and rushed down there. No one was in the big cellar, either. But as he took a step toward the stairs, he saw a flash of light pass by one of the small windows.

He hurried over to the window, stood on tiptoe, and peered out. A light blue convertible was being jockeyed into the garage and at the wheel was the girl who had invited him in. The Phantom hurried upstairs to the living room and sat down in the chair he had been occupying. Picking up the magazine, he appeared to be deeply engrossed in some article.

A good ten minutes more went by, and still the girl didn't appear. The Phantom was getting restless again when she walked into the living room. There was a half-smoked cigarette between her fingers.

"I'm terribly sorry," she said. "That was one of my friends on the phone. You know — the kind who never hangs up. Why, I must have been on the wire for half an hour at least."

"I hadn't noticed," the Phantom told her politely.

"I must apologize again," she went on, "for telling you Dad would be home soon. I had completely forgotten he told me he wouldn't be home until late. There's some sort of a business meeting —"

"About the television station in which he is interested?" the Phantom asked.

"Yes." She nodded. "He must have forgotten his appointment with you here. I wish I could reach him, but —"

The Phantom arose. "It's quite all right, Miss McLean. I can see him tomorrow. Tell him the man he asked Frank Havens to send, was here. I'll hold myself available until he gets in touch with me."

"I'm so sorry," she repeated, still apologetic. "I'll certainly tell Dad when he —"

A door opened somewhere upstairs. The Phantom heard it clearly and so did the girl. All the color in her cheeks drained out of her face. As he pivoted quickly he noted that the back of her suit — both the coat and skirt — seemed to be smeared with a gritty, rust-colored substance which he knew had not been there when she let him into the house.

There were footsteps on the second floor. They started down the stairs. The original of the oil painting which hung over the fireplace appeared in the doorway. His hair was rumpled, he wore slippers and a lounging robe, and he was blinking sleepily.

"Hello, Lisa," he said, and smiled at the girl.

"Why — Dad!" she exclaimed. "What on earth —"

He laughed. "You were out in back somewhere when I came home late this afternoon. I was exhausted so I lay down. I guess I must have been more tired than I realized. Only woke up this moment." He looked at the Phantom. "I'm sorry if I kept you waiting, sir. Is there anything special —"

The Phantom gave no indication that he knew both these people were liars. Neither had been in this house fifteen minutes ago.

"Quite all right, Mr. McLean," he said. "I had an appointment with you at nine-thirty, but if —"

McLean stiffened slightly, as if preparing himself for a shock.

"You are — Frank Havens' friend?"

"I am the Phantom Detective, Mr. McLean."

Lisa gave a startled gasp — and in it was more of fear than surprise.

McLean nodded heavily. "Please sit down again," he said. "I'm afraid I brought you all the way to this city for nothing."

The Phantom sat down. "But Mr. Havens particularly emphasized the fact," he murmured, "that you needed help. Badly and quickly."

"I thought I did," McLean said. "There were — well, certain factors I felt sure were operating against me. I was completely mistaken. I'm certain of that now. I'm deeply sorry I troubled you and Frank Havens. He's an old friend of mine. I knew, as everyone does, that not only is he also a good friend of yours, but your only personal contact, so when I mistakenly believed I needed help, I thought he might provide me with the best. Meaning, of course, you."

The Phantom arose slowly.

"All right, Mr. McLean. I'm glad whatever troubled you had cleared up. If anything happens to make you change your mind, I'll be at the Windmere Hotel for a time. I'm registered there under the name of Arnold King."

"Yes — yes, of course," McLean said. He seemed anxious for his visitor to leave. "You'll excuse me now. I missed dinner and I'm famished. If you'd care to stay —"

"No, thank you," the Phantom said. "Good night, Mr. McLean, and remember, I shall be glad to give you whatever help I can."

Lisa McLean hurried off, apparently to see about food for her father. McLean went with the Phantom to the front door and bade him good night. The Phantom drove slowly away, sorely perplexed as to what this was all about.

He reviewed what had happened. Lisa had received a phone call. Whoever had called must have told her something which made her slip out of the house, drive somewhere and return promptly. But why had she lied about it?

Her father just as surely had slipped into the house by a back door, used a rear stairway to reach his room and quickly changed into slippers and robe, then pretended he had been there all the time. Something had happened to make those two lie.

The Phantom had no suspicions that they had slipped away to commit any crime. Frank Havens had vouched for McLean, had asked the Phantom as a personal favor to come here and help the man. Havens picked his friends well. He wouldn't have been wrong about McLean.

CHAPTER II

THE MARK OF MURDER

FRANK HAVENS

As the Phantom reached the busier sections of town, he heard the wail of sirens, several of them. Soon two radio cars whined toward him from the opposite direction. These were followed by a black sedan, unmarked, but its siren raised an unholy din in the night. Following this came a sleek ambulance, red blinker lights flashing.

More on a hunch than anything else, the Phantom tramped on the brakes, turned around and began following the procession. The speeding cars roared around McLean's neighborhood and on for about two more miles.

Then, just ahead, the Phantom saw crimson lights, apparently suspended in the sky. But he recalled that during the day he had seen the steel skeleton of a television tower at this spot. Those crimson blinkers were simply warnings to planes.

The sirens started to moan down. By the time the Phantom reached the spot, headlights were flooding the base of the mammoth television tower. A dozen or more policemen were there, and an equal number of men in civilian clothes. They seemed to be gathered about something that lay on the ground.

The Phantom got out of his car and approached the group. A uniformed police sergeant suddenly grabbed his arm.

"Okay, mister," he said. "We can't have people tramping around here. Run along, like a good guy."

"What's happened?" the Phantom asked.

"If it'll ease your curiosity," the sergeant said, "somebody fell off that television tower and landed on the rocks. Believe me, you wouldn't like to see what's left."

"I think I would," the Phantom said.

Digging a hand under his coat, he took a small leather case from a secret pocket. He slipped this open and suddenly that small portion of the night around them was illuminated by a million flashing lights. For in that leather case was a platinum and diamond badge in the form of a domino mask. The badge of the Phantom Detective! And police officers, not only throughout this country but in many foreign lands, recognized and respected the significance of that emblem.

"The Phantom!" the sergeant said. "I'm mighty glad I've had a chance to meet you, sir — been hearing about you for many a long day. But it's like I told you — this is nothing for you. Far as we know now it's just some old bum who climbed up on the tower when nobody was looking and fell off it."

They walked toward the body and the sergeant broke through the crowd. The Phantom looked down at a grisly sight. There wasn't any question that this man had fallen from a great height. He lay face down, but his features would have been unrecognizable anyway. He had landed against large rocks which had been piled up during the excavation work necessary to install the base of the tower.

The man wore old, much-worn clothing. His shoes were scuffed and down at the heels. His hat, on the ground a dozen feet away, was battered and had a greasy ring beneath and above the frayed ribbon.

The Phantom sighed. Death was never something he could easily take. But this obviously was exactly what the sergeant had said — some bum who had fallen off the television tower. Why he had ever wanted to climb it was something for the police to determine. It had nothing to do with the Phantom.

An orderly from the ambulance was leaning against one of the tower girders and smoking a cigarette. He flipped the butt away, straightened up and started toward the ambulance. As he turned, headlights brought him into bold relief. The Phantom barely restrained a swift exclamation. For the back of the orderly's white coat was smeared with a gritty, rust-colored substance. Obviously it had come from the girder against which he had been leaning.

And — the back of Lisa McLean's coat and skirt had been covered with an identical substance!

Plainly, thought the Phantom, there was considerably more here than met the eye. Even if he heard no further word from Lisa's father, he decided he would not be in any great hurry to leave the city of Uncas — not until a few puzzling matters were explained to his satisfaction.

Often the Phantom, in one or another of the roles he created, admitted to being the world-famous detective, as he had in this town, but his real identity was known only to one man in the world. That man was Frank Havens, publisher of a string of newspapers from coast to coast, and the man who had been the closest friend of the Phantom's father, now dead. The single living human being who knew that the Phantom was, in fact, Richard Curtis Van Loan, supposed society playboy and wealthy idler, was Havens.

Van's choice of a life profession had not, however, come about through deliberate selection, but had been more or less a matter of chance. Born to wealth and a life of ease, he had been definitely bored with a do-nothing existence when Frank Havens, who had always watched over him with a father's care, had come up with a solution. He had suggested that Van try his hand at helping out his New York paper, the *Clarion*, in some routine work connected with a puzzling murder case. Van Loan had agreed, since Havens had put it rather as a favor to him.

Surprisingly — even to himself — Van had solved the case quickly. It had clearly come to him then — what to do with his life. For in that short time he had discovered a natural flair for detective work. With the usual energy he possessed in high degree, but which never before had been displayed except on the polo field or the tennis court, he had entered into his lifework with zest and determination.

Frank Havens had been almost as enthusiastic as Van himself. But when they plotted the bizarre career of the man who soon was to become known as the "Phantom Detective" — the name given to him by reporters on his first successful try, men who had no idea he was the wealthy and socially prominent Richard Curtis Van Loan — they had realized that as a measure of personal safety it would be better if Van continued his pose as a somewhat bored and ineffectual member of the idle rich.

Van immediately went into a strenuous training, and a thorough study of his new profession. One of his first chores was to master the difficult art of disguise. He resorted to no tricks like false whiskers, or the better known mechanical devices to change his appearance. Rather, he used simple dyes, different ways of combing his hair, different postures, methods of walking, and various changes in the slant of his eyes. He quickly reached a point where he actually lived the roles he created.

It was not long, once he considered himself sufficiently

prepared and had started out on his crime-hunting anonymously, before he became a well-known figure both to police and crooks. Criminals of all types hated and feared him. The minions of the law admired his work, helping him in every way possible, and always recognizing the gem-studded badge he carried. Because of its great intrinsic value there was little likelihood of that badge being duplicated.

It was to Van Loan's penthouse suite atop a tall apartment dwelling of the wealthy that the Phantom unobtrusively retired after his sorties, to again become the lackadaisical Van Loan. In that penthouse, which could be reached by a private entrance and a private elevator, he kept, in a hidden compartment, his makeup materials and other "tools of trade." He had a small lab there also, but maintained an elaborate one in New York's Bronx where he was known as "Dr. Bendix," a somewhat cranky stoop-shouldered old scientist. Dr. Bendix was supposed to have some sort of Government connections, and since he showed inclinations of preferring a hermit's life, he and his laboratory were left strictly alone by the none too curious few who lived near his somewhat dilapidated converted warehouse.

In keeping with his determination to learn everything connected with his profession, the Phantom had trained himself to mimic voices, to act his various roles to the hilt. He became a deep student of all forms of criminology, spending long hours in his Bronx crime library, which had no equal outside that of the F.B.I. in Washington. In fact, if his talents had bent in that direction, he would have made a formidable crook, because he knew all their tricks.

Sometimes, when the Phantom needed the aid of a clever woman in some case, he would call on Muriel Havens, the lovely daughter of the publisher. Muriel was always eager to help — and without the slightest suspicion that she was really helping Richard Curtis Van Loan, one of her best friends since childhood.

Another who eagerly aided the Phantom when called upon was a red-headed dynamo named Steve Huston, ace crime reporter for Frank Havens' New York *Clarion*. Huston was equally in the dark as to the Phantom's real identity, and never sought to ferret it out, being content that he could help the great anonymous detective.

Now, here in Uncas, on something that had been beginning to look like a wild goose chase, the Phantom was wondering if he would not have use for one or both of those loyal aides of his before long.

He had encountered all manner of crooks and criminals in his exciting career, but never before had he suspected the people he was supposed to help. Not when they were friends of Frank Havens. But now he was forced to doubt Chester McLean and his beautiful daughter, Lisa.

Havens might be able to explain some of this puzzle. Van's old friend had promised to come down and meet him here. So Van was not surprised when he let himself into his hotel room and found Havens already waiting for him.

Havens, white-haired, handsome, and a powerfully built man for his age, gave no indication that he knew the man who came into the room. Havens never recognized the Phantom while he was in disguise, until the Phantom gave the first recognition. In that manner Havens couldn't make a mistake and greet the wrong man. But he knew this man instantly now when Van touched an ear lobe, the given sign.

"I'm glad you're here, Mr. Havens." Van closed and locked the door. He threw his hat on the bed and sat down. "Things have happened and I can't begin to explain them."

Havens looked startled "But, Dick, what did McLean have to say?"

"Nothing. He told me he'd made a mistake and apologized for having you send me to him. . . Mr. Havens, have you any idea what this is all about?"

"Well, yes. Not too well, but I do know that McLean owns half of a television station here in town. He bought into it about three years ago."

Van Loan told Havens about how he had searched the McLean house, knew nobody was in it, and that therefore both McLean and his daughter had lied.

"I simply can't understand it," Havens commented ruefully. "In fact, I was surprised when McLean asked me to bring you into the case. McLean is the rough and tough type who likes to fight his own battles. When he called for help, I knew things must be in serious condition."

"Didn't he give you the slightest intimation as to what this was all about, Mr. Havens?"

"Well, he did say that the television station was running into some bad luck. Two men were killed while the tower was being built. Another was killed in the studio. Broadcasts have gone sour, actors up and quit without notice so that broadcasts have had to be called off. Name bands have been unaccountably delayed, missing their dates on this station. And a few hundred more minor mishaps, from broken wires and cables to missing props." Van nodded slowly. "So that's it. Tell me more about this TV station, Mr. Havens."

The publisher did not have a great deal of information, but he gave it.

"Well," he said, "it was started three years ago by a man named Alonzo Woodward. He began in a small way, purely local stuff. But television had been getting stronger and this station grew with it. McLean bought a half interest — cost him a lot of money, too."

"And all these difficulties began after McLean bought in?" Van asked.

"I think so, Dick. Though this intimidation has grown ever since it was learned the coaxial cable — that's the television network cable — was unexpectedly routed this way. This station will become one of the biggest after tomorrow night."

"What happens then?" Van Loan inquired.

"The station officially is welcomed into the big network. You recall how it was done in radio, a big program in honor of the new station."

"Mr. Havens," Van said, "I'm sure something is decidedly wrong at the McLean home. Mr. McLean, of course, would hardly confide in me. But you're one of his best friends."

Havens nodded. "You want me to see him, find out what this is all about and tell him again that you are ready to help?"

"You're the man to do it," Van said.

"All right." Havens arose. "I'll go see him right away. But I won't tell him about that rusty mark you spotted on Lisa's suit. The way McLean is acting, he must have enough worry on his mind without that.

"Good," Van Loan said. "I'll meet you back here. I'm going to have a talk with the local police authorities, then pay a little visit to the morgue."

"McLean wouldn't have gone to the police with his troubles," Havens reminded him.

"Perhaps not, but maybe they know about it. Or possibly this Alonzo Woodward filed some sort of a complaint. After all, it was his television station that it seems is being sabotaged."

"All right," Havens said. "Probably McLean was mistaken and there's nothing in this for you, Van. I'll try to find out."

CHAPTER III

A BUM WITH A MANICURE

STEVE HUSTON

Five minutes after Frank Havens had departed, the Phantom made his way to City Hall and the local police station. There he made himself known, and shortly was shaking hands with the burly, white-haired Chief of Police.

The Phantom sat down.

"It's come to my attention," he said, "that somebody has been trying to make a lot of trouble for this television station owned by Chester McLean and Alonzo Woodward. Do you have anything in your files on it, Chief?"

"We've got a nice fat file on it," the Chief declared. "But it won't help prove anything. Sure there have been a lot of accidents — and plenty that didn't look like accidents either, but we couldn't produce any evidence they weren't."

"I see. Have you any idea who may be responsible?"

"Any idea?" the Chief blurted. "Phantom, we *know!*"

"Interesting," the Phantom commented. "Are the details a secret?"

"They are not. Putting it simply, we have an ex-gangster living here, a fellow who made a lot of money from illicit enterprises that stem all the way back from prohibition days. This man wants that television station."

"An ex-gangster wants a TV setup?" the Phantom frowned.

"That's right. It's no secret that many gangsters, these days, with plenty of money and a little shaky from flirting with prison, have been trying to get into legitimate businesses, and are!"

"Yes," the Phantom admitted, "I know."

"That's what this Hugo Brennan is trying to do," the Chief said.

"Brennan?" the Phantom repeated softly. "He's a dangerous man, Chief."

"And a wealthy one. He went to Woodward first and asked

to buy in. Woodward refused. Brennan then tried to make a deal with McLean and that didn't work. So he's going to take over the station anyway. By first breaking it down until the owners will be glad to sell."

"The old intimidation racket was half-dead for a long time, Chief," the Phantom said. "We ought to finish it off — make it really dead."

The Chief shrugged. "We've tried. We've pestered Brennan with every device we know from parking tickets to ordinance infractions we'd overlook from anyone else. Nothing works. Brennan is here to stay. We can't drive him out of town."

"Maybe I could." The Phantom smiled a little.

"Then you have my blessing," the Chief said. "We don't like people of Brennan's stripe. And we don't like the kind of muscle men he has imported. Watch your step. Brennan doesn't scare."

"They all do," the Phantom said, "when you go at them the right way . . . Now what about this dead man found at the base of the television tower tonight?"

"Um — you know about that, eh? Well, we don't know who he is. No state fingerprint record. We've forwarded a copy of the prints to Washington. Not a thing on the body to identify. We can't even figure out why he ever tried to climb that tower."

"Did the autopsy show he'd been using intoxicants?" the Phantom asked.

"No — not a trace of alcohol or drugs," the Chief told him. "That's what threw us. You can expect anything from a drunk, but a sober man doesn't try to climb a nine-hundred-foot steel tower in the middle of the night."

"Could he have been one of Brennan's men, trying to sabotage the tower?" the Phantom suggested.

"With what? He didn't have so much as a nail file on him. He couldn't pry that tower apart with his bare hands."

"I see. Thanks, Chief. Do you mind if I go to the morgue and take a look at the dead man?"

"The morgue is right here in this building," the Chief said. "I'll take you there. Come on."

The Phantom was led down a long, dismal corridor, down a flight of narrow steps and into a small room equipped with four surgical tables. On one of these lay a covered form. The Chief called a white-coated man over and introduced him.

"This is Dr. Falkner. Doc, meet the Phantom."

The doctor whistled softly between his teeth. "Something tells me our unidentified friend here is assuming some importance. I'm glad to meet you, Phantom."

The doctor lifted the covering away. The Phantom looked down at the man he had last seen dead at the foot of the television tower. It was not a pleasant sight.

"Apparently when he fell from a great height his face was crushed by the rocks," Dr. Falkner said. "Death was instantaneous, of course."

"Doctor," the Phantom said slowly, "how long had he been dead before you examined him?"

"Perhaps four hours."

"Weren't you called in immediately after he was found?" the Phantom persisted.

"I was right here," Dr. Falkner said.

"But if he died four hours before that, it must have still been daylight when he fell," the Phantom said.

"Yes," Falkner admitted. "I still say he died four hours before I saw him.

The Phantom bent over the corpse. "When I saw him," he said, "he was dressed like a tramp. Yet his hands are clean and I think . . . Doctor, do you have a magnifying glass?"

Falkner nodded and went to a desk where he rummaged through drawers.

The Phantom studied the soles of the dead man's feet, and his heels.

"He certainly wasn't a man who walked a great deal or did any hard work," he decided. "He was accustomed to wearing good fitting shoes too. Not a bunion or a corn. No heel ridges."

Dr. Falkner handed the Phantom a magnifying glass. The Phantom held this over the dead man's fingernails, then called the doctor over.

"Take a look," he said. "Near the base of the fingernails. I'd suggest you scrape some of that substance off and analyze it. I'm sure you'll find it's a colorless nail polish. The kind that men have manicurists use on their nails."

"A bum with a manicure?" the Chief of Police blurted. "Phantom — keep digging. You're getting results."

The Phantom nodded. "His scalp is clean, his hair was cut by an expert and not long ago. Chief, I have a suggestion."

"I'm wide open to it. Shoot!"

"First of all we're reasonably sure this man was no tramp

and, because he was dressed like one, this case moves out of the accident class and into murder."

"How can a man be murdered by being dropped off a high tower?" the Chief demanded. "There's a narrow steel ladder. Only one man could go up it at a time and an intended murder victim wouldn't fall for any trick which could have got him thrown off."

"Maybe he would, if he trusted the man who was climbing the tower with him," the Phantom said. "However, I'm beginning to think this man was dead before he was dropped off the tower."

The Chief groaned. "And we had such a nice simple homicide case! Now it's murder — and not done through the guy falling onto those rocks."

The Phantom turned to Dr. Falkner.

"Suppose this man was dead when he was flung off that tower. If he had died only a short while before, could an autopsy tell the whole story?"

"No," Falkner admitted. "Not if he was thrown off only a few minutes after death. Say, within half an hour. There'd still be bloodstains. But you must be wrong, Phantom."

"Why?" the Phantom asked.

"Because if the fall off that tower didn't kill him, what did? I performed a post mortem. Death was caused by internal injuries and a skull fracture. No bullet holes, knife wounds, signs of throttling. No poison, smothering — nothing like that. He died as the result of a fall, Phantom. There isn't even a mark on the back of his head. Of course the front is caved in, but —"

The Phantom nodded. "You know your business, Doctor, and I'll take your word for it. Anyway, our first step is to find out who this man was. Chief, what do you think of the idea of calling in a physiologist who can rebuild this man's features in clay? I know of one you might call."

"That's the best idea yet," the Chief agreed. "I'll do that right away."

The Phantom wrote down a name and an address and gave this to the Chief.

"Let me know as soon as you learn anything about him," he asked. "Right now I want to pay Hugo Brennan a visit."

"He lives at 2230 Wildwood Road," the Chief said. "I thought you'd get around to that. Look — a word of warning. He keeps a stable of rough boys around that place. Hugo doesn't like people dropping in and there'll be a reception committee waiting to greet you."

"It should be interesting," the Phantom said mildly. "Thanks for the tip."

CHAPTER IV

THREAT OF DANGER

Hugo Brennan must have been born tough, raised tough, and had grown up to live with toughness. He was a tall man, with a deceptively serene face. Experience in the ring hadn't marked him physically, but he had learned by that how to stay trim. Even now, at nearly fifty, he had no surplus fat, and his coats were filled with shoulders, not padding.

He had assumed a swaggering walk when he had first become powerful and it had stuck with him. Even in the privacy of his big home he swaggered.

He came into the living room to answer the telephone which had been ringing shrilly. The room was dark, so he switched on the lights, picked up the phone and growled a greeting. There was no answer. He slammed the phone down in its cradle, muttering something about wise guys.

Then some intuition made him turn around slowly. In the further corner of the room sat a stranger, a man who was quietly studying him and making no move to arise.

Brennan almost lost his swagger as he walked toward the corner.

"Who the devil are you?" he demanded. "How'd you get in here?"

"Over your steel fence, Mr. Brennan," the Phantom said. "Then I used those French doors leading into your garden."

"Yeah?" Brennan cast a quick glance at a small table to his left. There was a gun in the drawer there. He moved casually toward it. "You greased somebody's palm," he accused. "I want to know who let you in."

"Your boys didn't even see me." The Phantom smiled. "I had an idea they might not let me through and I didn't want to tangle with them. So I merely slipped in here, dialed your own number on the telephone and hung up quickly after it rang. I had an idea it would bring you here."

"You did, huh?" Brennan scowled. "Well, I see who I want to see and them I don't get heaved out. So start moving."

"But you don't know why I came," the Phantom protested mildly. "You ought to be slightly interested."

"I'm not," Brennan snapped. He had reached the table and had one hand resting on it, just above the drawer. "Also, I happen to hate wise guys, and you strike me as being one."

"I'm sorry," the Phantom said. "It's because I'm not wise that I'm here. I want to know something, and I think you can tell me."

Brennan laughed. "You're no cop. I'd have a cop's badge for breaking into my house this way. You're no punk, because you don't talk or act like one. So I'm guessing you're a smart reporter and you want a story. I'll give you a story that'll knock your hat off."

Brennan yanked the drawer open, dipped a hand into it and began to search around for the gun. The Phantom lifted the hat which had been resting on his lap. Beneath it lay an automatic.

Is this what you re looking for?" he asked.

Brennan jerked erect, and there was a different look in his eyes.

"You're pretty good, chum. Suppose you let me in on the deal. And start off by telling me who you are — if you don't mind, of course."

"I don't, Brennan. They call me the Phantom."

Brennan's half-slitted eyes opened to their widest. His jaws clamped shut and a slow wave of red started climbing up his jowls. He finally laughed. There was no humor in it, unless it was directed at himself. He sat down opposite the Phantom.

"For a lot of years I been hearing about you," he said slowly. "I even hoped I'd run across you some day so I could show the boys you're not quite as smart as you're cracked up to be. As of right now, I think I'm glad we didn't meet."

"Thank you." The Phantom grinned. "It might have been interesting. . . . Brennan, why are you trying to take over the television station owned by Hugo Woodward and Chester McLean?"

Brennan leaned back, taking a deep breath.

"So that's it," he said. "Who blew the whistle for you? Woodward or McLean?"

"Perhaps neither one, Brennan. Perhaps I'm just interested in finding out why a mobster like you wants to take over a respectable business."

"Okay," Brennan said. "I've got nothing to hide. I made dough, plenty of it. But I'm done with the old ways. That don't mean I'm finished making money. Only I want to do it legit from here on."

"And when those men refused to sell out, you simply

adopted your old routine of worrying them until they give in?"

Brennan scowled. "What do you mean by that crack?"

"You know exactly what I mean," the Phantom replied. "Gangster methods. Intimidation, sabotage. Anything that will weaken the other fellow until he feels it's cheaper — and safer — to let you in."

"Let's see you prove I ever tried to scare those two guys into selling out to me," Brennan challenged.

"Maybe I will, Brennan. But mainly I want to know why you even attempted to buy a television station."

"I told you — I wanted to put my dough into something respectable. A guy who runs a television station meets a lot of important people. He goes places. That's what I want."

"You mean," the Phantom said, *"you'd* like to worm your way in, assume a certain amount of power and shake down the owners for all you could get out of them. It won't work, Brennan. I won't let it."

The gangster smiled thinly. "You or anybody else can't stop me. Not so long as I keep my fingers clean. It's not against the law to want to buy in on any business, and if you say I'm trying to muscle in, you've got to prove that or shut up."

"I'll prove it," the Phantom said quietly.

"Listen!" Brennan was just as quiet. "Being what I am, or what I used to be, I got reasons to hate you. Plenty of good guys I knew went up against you and they lost. That's because you had them on the run and you had cops to back you up. But with me — I don't run and cops can't back you unless there's been a crime committed. Well, there may be at that. It might even be murder. Your murder."

"We'll see." The Phantom arose and put the automatic on the table. "Thanks for the warning. At least I know what to expect — and from whom. Do I leave as I arrived? Or shall I walk out and surprise your vigilant boys?"

"Remember," Brennan warned, "you may wish you hadn't horned into this."

"Good night," the Phantom said. "I won't forget."

He walked to the front door, opened it and stepped out to the big porch. Two men suddenly materialized out of the gloom and stared at him with open awe. The Phantom pulled his hat down more firmly and nodded to the pair.

"Better not go in for awhile," he said pleasantly. "Hugo's a trifle put out. Good night."

Nobody stopped him as he walked down the driveway to the gate. He opened it, sauntered through it unmolested, and walked to where he had parked his rented car. He drove away at a moderate rate of speed, but he was much more puzzled than he would have admitted to Brennan.

The ex-gangster may have been trying to buy his way into the TV business, but if he'd done that openly, he would hardly dare begin the usual muscle procedure of forcing his way in. There was far more to this than Hugo Brennan and his crude methods. McLean knew the answers. The idea was to make him talk. Perhaps that would involve first removing whatever menace had silenced him and made him change his mind about asking for help, after he had phoned Frank Havens.

Havens might already have some of the answers if McLean had opened up. The Phantom drove straight back to the hotel. It was provided with a parking space at the rear, unattended and merely a courtesy for guests. He backed into a vacant spot, got out and turned to close the car door.

Two men came from around other parked cars with a swiftness that almost caught the Phantom off-guard. Only the crunching of the cinders gave him a scant alarm, and he whirled.

The men were rushing straight at him. One of them swung something that looked like a blackjack. It missed the Phantom's head, but crashed against one shoulder. The force of the blow and the excruciating pain it brought him, sent the Phantom to one knee.

The man with the sap raised it again, but this time it didn't land. The Phantom threw himself forward. Extended arms suddenly wrapped themselves around the thug's legs, just below the knees. Quick pressure sent the man crashing to the ground.

The other thug yelled something and a third man came out of the gloom. Apparently, this one had been slated to do lookout duty, but now he seemed to be needed. The Phantom leaped to his feet and started running. He dodged behind a parked car, passed by two more, and then ran between cars toward the center of the parking space.

One of the men had followed him. The other had circled, just as the Phantom expected he would. Suddenly this man saw the Phantom coming at him, as if intent on a head-on collision. The thug reached for his pocket about the time the

Phantom's fist hit him low on the throat. The man gave a strangling gurgle, raised his hands toward his throat, but they never got there. The Phantom's next punch connected with the upraised jaw. The fight was over.

The Phantom wheeled. Another man was coming his way, but slowly. Suddenly the Phantom broke into a run straight at the man, watching in case he went for a gun. But the thug had witnessed the finish of the first fight He turned and started to do some running himself, but the Phantom overtook him before he reached the alleyway beside the hotel.

An arm looped around the running thug's neck and brought him to a skidding stop. He was whirled about, shoved an arm length's distance away and a fist crashed against his face. He went down heavily and stayed there.

The Phantom went back to look for the man who had tried to sap him. He was gone. So was the one he had knocked out in his second encounter, and when he raced back to where he had left the third thug, that one also had vanished.

The Phantom rubbed his aching shoulder, winced and then grinned. At least they weren't going to let him have his own way all through this. And it proved that Brennan was in it deep. Perhaps right up to his chin.

The Phantom walked warily to the front of the hotel, passed through the lobby and took the elevator to his floor. He saw the door to his room slightly ajar. He pushed it open, tense and ready for trouble if it waited. Frank Haven was alone in the room. He had a large piece of paper in his hand.

"I found this under the door when I got here a few minutes ago," he said. "It sounds like a threat of some kind."

Van took the paper. There were four crudely printed words on it:

SEE WHAT I MEAN

"It was meant to be a threat," Van said, as he put the warning down, "but it fizzled slightly. However, being on the receiving end of it offers some good food for thought, Mr. Havens. I've just seen a man named Brennan, a mobster who is supposed to have retired, but somehow I don't think he has. He sent three of his men to teach me a lesson. They did — that from now on I must be twice as careful. But how did Brennan know I occupied this room?"

"You've been around," Havens said. "Perhaps you told

someone and the word was passed along."

"Sure it was," Van agreed. "But I'm here under a name I made up on the spur of the moment when I registered. I'm not known by sight so I couldn't have been picked out. It's true I have been around town and talked to several people, but I told only one — no, two — persons the name under which I was registered."

"Perhaps then. . . You've found some sort of a clue," Havens suggested.

"Those two people, who know me by the name of Arnold King, happen to be Chester McLean and his charming daughter, Lisa."

Havens sat down heavily. "Dick, I've got a shock for you. Ten minutes after you left McLean's house, he packed a bag. Then he went to various places where he is known — a drug store, tobacco store, a few friends. He cashed checks for as much as these people could spare. Then McLean disappeared."

"What about Lisa?" the Phantom asked quickly.

"If she has the slightest idea of where he has gone, or why, she's a perfect actress."

"If he went of his own accord, he's a fool," Van declared. "All he's doing is pointing a finger of guilt at himself. I don't know what's due to break in this city, but it's going to happen soon and it will involve McLean."

"I still stand behind him," Haven said slowly. "I've known him a long time, Dick. If he ran away, he had a mighty good reason — and it wasn't for any purpose of self-protection. You're right — something is going to break!"

CHAPTER V

NO HELP WANTED

Although it was almost one in the morning, Alonzo Woodward answered his telephone promptly when the Phantom called from the lobby of the apartment house where the television man lived. Woodward asked him to come right up.

The station owner occupied a luxurious big apartment on a high floor. He was in the doorway when the Phantom walked swiftly down the corridor.

Woodward was a rotund man with red cheeks, bald head, and bright blue eyes. His handclasp was soft, flabby.

"Come in, come in," he said affably. "I don't know how the Phantom ever came to involve himself in this mess in Uncas, but I'm mighty glad to see you."

The Phantom sat down in a chartreuse-colored chair. Woodward apparently liked bright, modern furnishings. The Phantom refused a drink and plunged straight into his reason for calling.

"I understand that Chester McLean owns half of this television station here, Mr. Woodward."

"He does," Woodward admitted. "I began it, in a rather small way when television was just getting its start. I didn't have the money to build it into the kind of a station it deserved to be, so I went to McLean and he was forward-minded enough to see what this could be developed into."

"Tell me," the Phantom urged, "did this sabotaging begin right after McLean bought into the firm?"

"No," Woodward said. "Not for two years. We had been operating an unpretentious little affair — used local talent but did rather well. Then the lightning struck. They branched an arm of the transcontinental cable off in this direction and we became a big and important station overnight. That is, we will be big and important after tomorrow night, when we premiere our first network programs."

"But when did this series of accidents actually begin?" the Phantom asked.

"Right after we learned about our unexpected luck. When that cable made this station increase in value perhaps a dozen times."

"Do you think McLean has been trying to scare you out so

he can take over the whole thing?"

"No," Woodward answered curtly. "I'd trust McLean with anything."

"McLean has disappeared," the Phantom said. "And rather hastily, too."

Woodward shook his head. "I don't care what he's done. McLean is honest, and I'll stand back of him no matter what happens. I know McLean. Anyway, it's obvious who is causing this trouble."

"Meaning Hugo Brennan?" the Phantom queried.

Woodward nodded. "Yes, I mean Brennan. The likes of him have no business entering anything as big as television. He's a crook. He made his money by violence and he won't run a TV station any more honestly."

"Did he proposition you and McLean?" the Phantom went on.

"Did he? A dozen times. At first he was pleasant enough. All he wanted was a piece of the business. We refused and he became more insistent. He hinted we might be sorry if we didn't cut him in. Finally we told him not to bother us again, and that was when he showed what he really was. A blustering, threatening crook."

"And it seems he has carried out his threats," the Phantom said musingly.

"Yes, I suppose he has. You know of those so-called accidents we've had. But the other things — the small stuff — there's been so much of that we can't even begin to figure out which was deliberate. And frankly, I'm scared stiff at what may happen tomorrow night when we officially join the network."

"And Brennan is the only man you suspect of trying to wreck your station?" the Phantom asked.

Woodward hesitated, as though uncertain whether to say more.

"There is a man named Gordon Pulver," he finally admitted. "I hate to say anything about things I'm not sure of, or make accusations. But Pulver has been operating a radio station in town for years. Everyone expected he would start television, when it finally came into being. But I beat him to it."

"And Pulver resented it?" the Phantom asked.

"He became pretty ugly about the whole thing. I filed with the Federal Communications Commission first. My claim to the television station here took precedence. There wasn't room for two of them. Not at that time, and now that the cable is being connected with my station it makes ours more important than ever. Pulver went into a rage about the whole thing. He said I'd be sorry."

"And you expect trouble at your premiere network broadcast?" the Phantom asked.

"If they are going to strike at me, that will be the time to do it," Woodward sighed. "Phantom, will you attend the opening? I'll pay any reasonable fee you demand."

"I'll be there without fee," the Phantom said. "But getting back to McLean. His running away at this moment, when his station joins the network, means that something important must have happened. Have you any suggestions?"

Woodward shrugged. "Frankly — though I still don't believe it — Hugo Brennan must be responsible. He must have frightened McLean away. There's no other answer."

"Yes," the Phantom agreed somberly.

"It looks like that might be it. Perhaps Brennan figures he can deal with one man better than with two. But I wish I knew what he had on McLean. I can't see McLean getting so scared he'd run out."

Woodward stared at the rug in deep thought. Then he looked up.

"Why don't you talk to his daughter, Lisa? They are close. Whatever McLean has done, it must be with her knowledge and approval. They never have had any secrets between them."

The Phantom arose. "I think I'll take your advice, Mr. Woodward, and thanks. I'll be at your station tomorrow night and if there is anything I can do, just call on me."

Woodward saw him to the door, shook hands and watched the Phantom walk to the elevators. On the street, the Phantom got into his rented car and pulled away from the curb. He was trying to think this out, but there seemed to be no answer. Not even a direction in which the case headed.

Outwardly, the whole thing seemed simple enough. Brennan was an ex-gangster who usually got what he wanted by one means or another. He wanted this television station. Sabotage, intimidation and the disappearance of McLean all fitted into the pattern which Brennan would create. Yet the Phantom was not satisfied. There was something more, something that lay deep beneath the surface and refused to be dragged out.

Half a dozen blocks from Woodward's apartment, the Phantom began to use evasion tactics. Brennan would likely have him trailed, and expertly, too. But the Phantom knew all the tricks connected with that business. He sped up, made several quick turns, doubled back, stopped short and tried every means of determining whether or not he was being followed. After half an hour of this he was sure Brennan had not yet put his shadows on the job.

The Phantom headed for Lisa McLean's home.

The house was illuminated and, when he drove up to the front, the door opened instantly, and Lisa stepped out onto the porch. She showed her disappointment when the Phantom climbed the steps and approached her.

"My — my father isn't home," she said.

"I know, Miss McLean. I know a great deal, and I think we ought to compare a few notes. May I come in?"

She nodded dully. The Phantom entered the living room with her and took the same chair he had occupied so long during the early evening when he had waited for McLean to put in an appearance.

She sat down opposite him. Her eyes were cloudy with worry. Her hands, clasped tightly on her lap, showed white at the knuckles. Her breathing was short, nervous. The Phantom recognized these symptoms. Lisa McLean was in the grip of nearly complete panic terror.

"Do you want to tell me about it?" he asked quietly.

She bit her lower lip and looked up. "I don't know what you mean."

"I'm afraid you do. Your father ran away. Why?"

"No," she said in sharp rejection. "He's just off on a business trip."

"Then we can get hold of him easily enough," the Phantom said. "Where did he go?"

"I — don't know."

"Lisa McLean" — the Phantom leaned forward a little — "I'm on your side in this. Your father is a friend of Frank Havens and that makes him my friend. Mr. Havens is determined to stand behind your father — and so will I. But I must know the facts. Many of them I understand — how, for instance, Hugo Brennan is trying to muscle in and is using his old fashioned but effective tactics. But Brennan can be battled to a standstill if I don't have to work in the dark."

"I can't help you!" Lisa cried. "I tell you I can't!"

"Has Brennan threatened you?"

"No. No, I've never even seen Brennan. Please let me alone! I've had enough."

"I'm afraid I can't," the Phantom told her frankly. "You see, when I was here in this house early last night, you slipped away from the house and you were gone quite some time. Then your father came downstairs and explained that he'd been having a nap in his room. Both of you lied — you, by inferring you'd been on the telephone all that time I waited."

She raised her head high. "How do you know all this? How can you be so sure?"

"Because I looked," the Phantom said simply. "When people call me in, they're often in danger, and when I found myself in an empty house, I wondered if something had happened. So I checked the house from attic to cellar. I even saw you drive back, and your father was not in his room, as he said he was."

She looked straight at the Phantom. "I can't talk about it. Do you understand that? I can't talk about anything. If you want to help Dad and me — stay away from us. Forget Dad ever asked your help. He doesn't want it now, and neither do I."

The Phantom didn't arise. "Lisa," he said softly, "did you see your father kill the man we found at the foot of the television tower? Or did he see you kill him?"

For a moment he thought she was going to faint. The color ebbed from her face, leaving the rouge garish and ugly. She fought to retain possession of her sense, and the clamor of the phone helped more than anything else. She went off to answer it, but this time she didn't close the door. Whoever it was, her conversation was brief and limited mostly to listening. But when she came back to the living room, she was changed. Her eyes glowed and she seemed at ease.

"I'm sorry, Phantom," she said. "I know I was abrupt. I also know you can be trusted, but there is really nothing I can tell you. And of course, that talk about a killing was only to frighten me, to force me to answer your questions. I would gladly help you if I could. But don't you see? There is nothing to tell."

"All right," the Phantom said. "You know best, but please

don't hesitate to let me know if you do need help."

Outside, the Phantom drove away from the house, but he didn't travel far. He stopped and shut off the lights at a spot where he was high enough to overlook the McLean home and driveway.

As he expected, soon the garage lights flashed on and a big sedan was backed out fast. He never doubted but that Lisa was at the wheel and he was pretty sure she was answering some sort of a summons which had reached her through that phone call she had received.

From the way she had relaxed after it, the Phantom had an idea she had heard from her father. Perhaps she was going to meet him now. If she was, she was going to have company.

CHAPTER VI

HILLTOP HOUSE

LISA McLEAN

Lisa McLean headed toward town and drove straight through the deserted main street. The Phantom had to take elaborate precautions to prevent her from realizing she was tagged. He stayed as far behind as he dared and when they left the busier part of town, he promptly shut off his headlights before turning a corner which Lisa had taken.

Lisa sent her big car toiling up a steep incline. One side of this city was bordered by a long, high hill and she seemed to be headed for the ridge.

Now the going became even harder. Without lights, over unfamiliar roads, the Phantom was compelled to drive more slowly than he would have liked and the distance between his car and Lisa's grew greater. Then, suddenly, the tail-light of her car vanished. The Phantom hastily braked to a stop. Here, atop this ridge overlooking the city sprawled out below, was a single building. It stood starkly silhouetted against a dark sky.

It was four stories high, square and ugly. It had many windows, most of them heavily barred, and the roof was flat. The place seemed to be not only abandoned but badly run-down.

The Phantom backed his car off the road, behind thick brush, and made certain it could not be easily seen. Then, on foot, he moved rapidly toward that weird building. Nearing it, he saw Lisa's car parked at the rear. The door beside the driver's seat was still open, as if she had been in too much of a hurry to bother closing it.

The Phantom making sure of the automatic under his arm, scanned the darkness and listened carefully for sounds of anyone being close by. Finally he approached the rear door. It was not locked. He opened it silently, stepped inside, and smelled the dank mustiness of a building left unlived in to disintegrate.

He took a small flashlight from his pocket and risked

spraying the beam ahead of him. He saw that he was at the foot of a long corridor lined with closed doors. Everything was dust-ridden.

Then he heard Lisa's high heels clicking somewhere on the floor above. And he heard her voice calling:

"Dad! Dad, where are you? Dad — it's Lisa."

The Phantom slowly drew his gun. He didn't know what to expect as he moved forward slowly and with that quietness he had long ago developed. Some unique sense seemed to inform him of every board which would squeak, and he avoided these. Reaching the stairway, he started up it.

He didn't like this. There was something wrong with the whole affair and murder already had come into this strange game. He had a feeling that murder would come once more — perhaps many more times. His finger remained tight on the trigger.

"Dad!" Lisa was calling, a note of desperation in her voice. "Dad — where are you? I've brought the car. Dad!"

The Phantom stepped into view from one of the doorways. Lisa, at the far end of the hall, was using a flashlight, but she didn't aim the beam toward the Phantom and had no idea he was there. She took the next flight to the third floor and hurried along it, calling her father.

By the time the Phantom caught up with her again she was on the fourth and top floor. She was no longer calling, though, but sobbing. The Phantom realized now that whatever message bad brought her here was only a ruse. Her father wasn't here and likely never had been. The Phantom called her name.

Instantly the flashlight slashed his way, held him in its glare. Then Lisa snapped it off and leaned weakly against the dusty wall. The Phantom hurried to her.

"I'm sorry I had to follow you," he said. "But if your father had sent for you, I wanted to see him, too."

"He isn't here," she said dully. "And I'm glad — now. You'd have arrested him."

"I can't arrest anybody," the Phantom told her gently. "I wanted to talk to him because there are a lot of people in town who either do think — or soon will — that he murdered that man who was found at the foot of the television tower. I think your father could explain that to me. I think you could, too."

"I told you, it's impossible," she said. "Take me away from here — please!"

"Of course," he said. "But would you mind telling me who

telephoned that your father would be here?"

"I don't know who it was, Phantom. Just a man who said Dad had paid him to call me."

The Phantom frowned. "There must have been some reason for bringing you here. This is an isolated spot. Anything could happen, and I'm not sure —"

Abruptly he stopped and threw a protecting arm around the girl. In a whisper he warned her to be quiet. Somewhere in this old building there were telltale squeaks. That meant intruders, trying to be quiet but not entirely succeeding.

The Phantom guided Lisa toward one of the rooms. The door was open and they entered. He closed the door almost all the way, then drew one of his automatics.

"We'll get out of this," he assured her. "But as I expected, this was a trap for you."

"For me? But why, Phantom? Why?"

"I don't know — yet. What sort of building is this anyway?"

"It's an abandoned isolation hospital. They used it long ago, when there was a smallpox scare in town. Phantom, who is coming? Why do they want me?"

"I told you I don't know," he said.

His flashlight sprayed the room and showed the pile of ancient mattresses stacked almost to the ceiling and filling half of the room.

The intruders were on their floor now, and no longer trying to remain quiet. The Phantom could not distinguish the muttered words, but none of the men was on the move. Then some kind of a powerful searchlight suddenly made the corridor dazzlingly bright. A man's voice called out a command.

"Phantom! We know you're on this floor. Come out with your hands up. Way up!"

The Phantom signaled Lisa to remain quiet, though he had barely restrained a mutter of surprise himself when he heard his name called. How did anyone know he was here?

"Phantom," the same man called, "if we have to come after you, the girl may get killed. Be sensible. There are six of us. You can't get away, and all we want are some answers to a few questions."

The Phantom remained deadly quiet. He was weighing his chances. They seemed slim. This was one of the last rooms down the hall. The only stairway was blocked by those men and they would be armed and ready to kill. The Phantom was not deceived by their trick of making him reveal himself on the assumption that all they wanted were answers to questions. A setup like this was meant for murder.

Lisa put her lips close to his ear. "What are we going to do?" she asked.

He shook his head and then, realizing that wasted minutes might mean the difference between life and death, he let go of her and stayed close to the wall where the floor boards wouldn't squeak as he made his way to the single window.

He tried to raise it, but the window was stuck fast with the decay of age. There was nothing to do but force it. He used the heels of his palms and jarred the window loose. Then he raised it quickly.

That made enough noise to give away his approximate location and he knew those men would lose no time in scurrying toward the room. He raced to the door, pulled it wide and boldly stepped into the hallway. Both guns were in his hands, and both flamed. The powerful searchlight winked out to the accompaniment of crashing glass and the scream of someone who got nicked.

The Phantom dodged back into the room.

"Stay inside!" he warned Lisa. "Keep listening. If they steal this way, let me know."

He returned to the window and risked looking out and down. A jump would only result in broken limbs. He saw, however, that the building overlooked the city. Street lights made a pleasing pattern in the valley below, but they could have been a million miles away for all the good they would do him.

He twisted his head and peered up. The edge of the roof could be reached easily by standing on the window sill, but escape to the flat roof wouldn't place them in a more advantageous spot. In fact, they might be worse off.

"Phantom!" Lisa called "They're coming!"

He sped toward the door. He didn't have to show himself. Anybody in that corridor was a fair and easy target even though all he did was thrust an arm beyond the doorway and start blasting. The stealthy steps became noisy ones as the men scampered back. But not far. They simply dodged into some of those convenient rooms.

"We can't hold them off indefinitely," the Phantom said. "There must be some way to get help — or scare them off."

Grimly he regarded the stack of mattresses. He hurried

over to them and hauled one down. It was filled with cheap straw. The ticking was old and gave way when he ripped at it with a fingernail He quickly returned to Lisa.

"We've got to work fast and take chances," he said. "It's the only way. Those men are out to kill both of us. They must have known I'd follow you here. Are you game to take a long shot?"

"Anything, Phantom," she said. "Anything!"

"Good. I'm going to throw a few more slugs to keep them off for a few minutes. You drag two of those mattresses over to the window. Work fast!"

He moved to the door, waited until he heard the men on the move, then fired four fast shots along the corridor. Nobody was hit but by the sound of their scampering, they had all ducked for cover. The Phantom ran across the room. Lisa already had one mattress near the window and was dragging over a second one.

The Phantom moved close to her. "I'm going to try to reach the roof. They didn't bother to cover the outside of the building, so I ought to make it. As soon as I do, fold those mattresses and pass them up to me. It won't be easy, but it has to be done."

"I'll do my best," she promised. "But what good will mattresses do?"

"Maybe none at all, but it's our only chance," the Phantom said. "Wait a minute while I see if they're any closer."

He sped toward the door and hastily signaled Lisa to take cover. She jammed her slim form between the wall and the pile of mattresses. One of the gunmen was just outside the door. The Phantom clubbed his gun, raised it high and waited.

With a yell, the man came surging into the room. He had taken only a single step before the Phantom whipped the gun down. It was a well-aimed blow and caught the man on the back of the head, just below his hat. He didn't make a sound as he pitched forward.

The Phantom scooped up the fellow's gun, leaped to the door and fired a shot into the opposite wall. Others, who were edging closer, started for various rooms. One of them didn't quite make it. The Phantom leaped into the corridor and emptied the gun he had taken from the thug.

He heard a man's body strike the corridor wall under the impact of a slug, heard him slide to the floor. That would hold them a few more seconds.

He raced for the window and, with hardly a pause, worked his way through it, managed to get a foothold on the sill and raised himself. As his hands found the edge of the roof, he swung out and hoisted himself up. Then he was on the roof and squinting through the gloom to make certain nobody had been posted there. The roof was clear.

He lay prone, let his arms dangle down and at a hissed order, Lisa forced one of the thin mattresses out the window. It must have taken all her strength, but she managed to raise it until the Phantom could seize a corner and yank it upwards.

Within two minutes after he went through the window, the second mattress was on the roof and Lisa was clambering out of the window. She raised her hands. He grasped her wrists tightly and she swung out. He raised her swiftly and the next moment they paused to regain their wind.

"Thanks, Lisa," he said. "That took courage, and you've got plenty."

She shuddered. "Courage doesn't enter this scheme of things, Phantom. It was get out of that room or be killed. I'd have jumped if necessary. And — and I was wrong. I should have told you everything. I will."

"Later," the Phantom told her. "Right now I've got another job. They'll soon be inside that room and know where we've gone. They'll try to come up here and if there are enough of them, maybe they will. Some may try that roof hatch, but I can stop them there, unless others come through windows as we did and keep me so busy I can't stop them all."

"What can I do?" Lisa begged. "And these mattresses . . . I don't understand."

"Rip both of them open, pile up the straw. Here — take this pack of matches. When you have a good-sized stack of straw, set it on fire!"

"But Phantom," she gasped, "what good will that do us?"

CHAPTER VII

SIGNAL FIRE

Watching the hatch, the Phantom was listening for any sound which might tell him at what point along the roof edge to expect visitors.

"This building is in plain sight of the whole city," he called to Lisa. "If we start a good, bright fire someone is bound to see it and notify the Fire Department. If they get here in time, or if anybody shows up, well have a chance. Otherwise we fight it out from where we stand."

"I'll get busy right away," Lisa said grimly, now that she understood.

"This roof is as fireproof as a roof can be," the Phantom told her. "I don't believe we'll set the building on fire, making the fire up here. But we have to take a chance." His foot scraped the roof top and he bent down to study it in the ray of his flash. "It's cement, overlaid with some kind of gravel. It won't burn, kid! Get going!"

Suddenly the glass inset of the roof hatch crashed, and someone put a shoulder to the hatch itself. But it must have been stuck fast. This was the first real break in the Phantom's favor. He leveled his gun and sent a bullet through the shattered hatch, thanking his stars for the belt around his waist, and for his pockets in which was plenty of ammunition. The pounding on the hatch stopped instantly, then there was nothing but a lot of silence which he didn't like, He kept turning slowly, his eyes watching the roof edges on all four sides of the building.

A scraping noise alerted him. He spun around. Two hands were clawing at the edge of the roof. He rushed to the spot and slammed his gun muzzle down on one hand. Somebody howled in pain, and the man's other hand slid off the roof.

The Phantom did not hear a body crash to the ground, so he guessed that the man must have been held up by one of his pals. But if they kept trying that trick, while one or two of the others were at the hatch, waiting to take advantage of the Phantom's occupation of getting rid of the others, there would be a good chance for some one of them to get a shot at him.

Lisa was working fast. Shaking straw out of the mat-

The Phantom leveled one of
his guns and fired twice
(CHAP. VII)

tresses, she kicked it into a pile. Already one mattress was
empty and she was ripping the second one open.

A gun flamed through the hatch. At that moment, Lisa was
an open target, but the gunman was aiming at the more elu-
sive form of the Phantom — and he missed by a yard. The
Phantom's gun answered and there was no more of that for
the moment.

"All set!" Lisa called. "Here goes the match!"

She struck it, applied the tiny flame and the dry, aged straw
almost exploded. She leaped back and threw the empty mattress covers onto the blaze. It lit up the roof and almost seemed
to light up the whole sky. The Phantom nodded in satisfaction.
Now, if only someone in the city happened to look this way,
there would be help coming soon.

He rushed over to her and drew her toward the rather
doubtful protection of a flat chimney. They hugged it, both
watching the edges of the roof and the hatch.

One of the thugs took a long chance and emptied his gun
through the hatch, but he was shooting against the fire and his

targets were behind it. The light of the flames allowed them to hide well. Two of the killer slugs nicked the chimney. The Phantom leveled one of his guns, fired twice. Then he quickly knelt, hauled more clips from his pocket and reloaded both weapons.

Above the crackle of the fire, he heard a car motor sing into life. The besiegers had realized the flames might draw police and firemen and they wanted no part of any such reinforcements. The Phantom slid over to the edge of the roof and looked over.

Car headlights were switched on. Two men, carrying a third between them, lumbered toward the car and stowed their wounded pal inside. They ran back to the house after another wounded man who could navigate but had to be supported. All climbed into the car and it pulled away with a whine of too hastily applied gears.

The Phantom relaxed and went back to the chimney. "It's all right now," he told Lisa. "They've gone, but we'll be careful anyway. Let's start putting out this fire...."

Within minutes, the Phantom and Lisa McLean themselves were driving away. Fire apparatus was just reaching the scene, so that the Phantom was reasonably certain no killers would be lurking in the darkness waiting for them.

"We won't bother to stay and explain that fire," he told Lisa, with a grin. "There would be too many questions. Those thugs got their wounded away and all the firemen will find are bullet holes in the walls — if they look hard enough."

Lisa was staring straight ahead. "Phantom," she said soberly, "I was silly not to have trusted you fully right from the first. Now I want to tell you the truth."

"Good," he approved, "I've been waiting for that."

She plunged right into it.

"That night you came to meet Dad by appointment," she said, "you were right. I did slip out of the house and — and Dad did lie when he came downstairs and said he'd been taking a nap."

"I know that," the Phantom said. "But I'd like to know why you both lied."

"I don't know exactly what happened," Lisa said slowly. "Before this, Dad never held back anything from me, but lately he — well, he changed. He seemed to be afraid. I'm sure it must have been because of this man Brennan and those thugs who work for him."

"That's an opinion shared by others," the Phantom admitted. "Go on."

"That night. . . well, I left you alone in the house after someone phoned me. He told me my father wanted me at the foot of the television tower. I was to go there without telling a soul — and I did. When I got there, I — I saw Dad bending over this — dead man. He must have heard me, and without knowing who I was, he ran away. Of course I didn't know the man was dead until I got close to him. At first I was afraid I hadn't seen Dad at all and that it was he who lay face down on the rocks. But — but of course it was only this stranger."

"Then you leaned against the tower," the Phantom said. "And you got the back of your suit covered with a telltale smear of rust. I saw it when you returned home, and later I found out where it came from."

"But you didn't tell anyone," she said, in a surprised voice. "Why, Phantom?"

"Because I trusted your father, and that meant I also trusted you. Anyway, I wanted time to see what this was all about. . . Now — why did your father run away?"

"I don't know," she confessed seriously. "Unless he had been threatened, and went off so that — that I wouldn't be in danger too."

"I doubt it," the Phantom said. "Because you were in danger, anyway. I wish I knew who those men really were after in that old hospital. Me — or you."

"It must have been me," she said. "I was there because I'd had a phone call. Though I honestly can't give you any reason why anybody would want to kill me."

"This dead man you saw at the base of the tower," he said. "Had you ever seen him before?"

"No. I don't think so. He was so horribly crushed it was hard to tell. But he was dressed like a tramp and I'm certain he was a total stranger."

The Phantom suddenly changed the subject. "What do you know about Alonzo Woodward?" he asked. "The man from whom your father bought a half interest in this television station."

"Not much, Phantom. He seems nice. Dad likes him, and so do I. I don't think he had much when he started the station, but he certainly expanded and advanced it."

"Where did he come from?" the Phantom asked.

"I really don't know," she said with a puzzled expression.

"He never talked much about himself, though I think I've heard him say he was once in business in New York . . . Phantom, why are you asking me all these questions about Mr. Woodward?"

The Phantom shrugged.

"Because Woodward suggested I talk to you," he said. "When I got to your home, you received this phone call which brought you to the old hospital. If Woodward had planned that, he would have known I would follow you — and those men with the guns and determination certainly knew I was there, without actually seeing me."

"But why would Mr. Woodward do such a thing?" she asked impulsively. "After all, you're helping him. It's his television station that seems to be drawing all these crooks. Woodward wants to keep it. He's said he'd fight anybody who tried to take it away, and he defied Brennan who was all set to try it."

"Yes, I know," the Phantom admitted. "I'm probably wrong about him, but I think he might explain a few things."

"May I ask a question for a change?" Lisa said.

The Phantom nodded, and she said promptly:

"Do you know why Dad ran away?"

"I'm afraid I do," he told her. "There could be three reasons. One — he was afraid of Brennan, which I doubt. From what I know of your father, he'd fight it out."

"I'm sure he would! And the second reason?"

"He actually did kill the man we found at the foot of the tower. However, that I also discount. There's no motive."

"And the third reason?"

"It's the one in which I have the most faith, Lisa, and it's not a pretty reason. You went to the tower. You saw a man you believed to be your father hovering over a corpse. But what if it wasn't your father? What if he came along later — and saw you there with the dead man? Perhaps he thought you had killed him."

"But why would that make him run away?" she demanded.

"He might be accepting the blame so none of it will be aimed your way, Lisa. That theory makes sense, except for one thing. If you didn't know the dead man, why did your father think you killed him? Something must have happened just before the crime."

"I — thought it was just an accident," she said nervously.

"I believed the man was some tramp who was intoxicated and had tried to climb the tower for no special reason."

"It was murder," the Phantom said. "I'm sure of it, just as I'm certain the dead man was no bum. And finding out who he really is happens to be my first job. Meanwhile I'm going to send you away."

"Oh, Phantom, I can't go! What if Dad returns or wants me?"

"If you stay here, he may come back to find a dead daughter," the Phantom reminded her grimly. "You've got to do as I say, Lisa McLean. We'll go home while you pack a bag. Then I'm putting you on a plane for New York. At the airport, I'll arrange to have Muriel Havens — Frank Havens' daughter — meet you. You'll like her and you'll be safe with her.

Lisa nodded and sighed. "Whatever you say, Phantom. I know now that you think straight, and that not trusting you before almost cost me my life. I'll do exactly as you tell me."

CHAPTER VIII
DEAD MAN'S IDENTITY

Some two hours later, after carefully scanning the passengers on an east-bound plane, the Phantom watched it take off with Lisa aboard. He felt better when the ship was airborne and vanishing in the night sky. He was tired, but there were things to do and he drove straight to Police Headquarters.

There he found a college-trained scientist on night duty in the police laboratories. He gave the Phantom the medical examiner's report, but it showed only that the dead stranger had died from the results of a terrific impact after a long fall.

The young sergeant in charge of the lab lit a cigarette and leaned back in his chair.

"Have you made any progress, Phantom?" he asked.

"Not much, Sergeant, I'd like to examine the dead man's clothing next."

"I took care of that detail," the sergeant said, smiling. "I also got wind of the fact that you didn't think this man was alive when he hit those rocks at the foot of the television tower."

"I don't think so," the Phantom said flatly. "But I've got to prove it."

"I vacuumed the dead man's clothing," said the youthful officer. "I got some good samples of cement dust — old cement that was impacted clear through the cloth. I've seen that before, when someone jumped out of a window and landed on a cement courtyard."

"Ah!" The Phantom nodded. "We're getting somewhere."

"Sure," the sergeant said a little wryly. "All we have to do is find out what window he was pushed out of and what courtyard he smacked. There must be several thousand windows and an awful lot of courtyards in this town,"

"But if we know he was dead when he was dropped off the tower, we have something," the Phantom said. "How about his shoes? The tower ladder was rusted. If he climbed it, there should be traces of rust, shouldn't there?"

"I looked for that and there were none, Phantom. That guy never climbed the tower. He was carried up it, then dropped. Whoever did that worked fast. After the guy was killed by smacking into that cement courtyard, or whatever it was he hit, his body was quickly transported to the tower. Before the blood congealed much."

"You're right up-to-date here," the Phantom said approvingly. "Now let's study what we've got. First — the dead man is obviously a stranger. His description, except for that of his face, has been printed in the newspapers. It's a little too early to be certain, but if he was known here, don't you think someone would have come forward and made an attempt to identify him?"

"Maybe," the sergeant admitted.

"What about dental work, scars, moles — things like that?"

"He had some fillings and a small fixed bridge, but the work wasn't done here in town. We made up a dental chart and circulated it fast so we know. No scars or other marks . . . And oh yes — Washington says his prints aren't on file. The State Police report the same thing."

"So we can still assume he was a stranger in town," the Phantom said. "Which means he may have been staying at a hotel. Now a man who has his nails professionally manicured, won't stay at a flop house and you don't have too many first rate hotels in Uncas. If we stroll around to all of them and find one where a guest has been mysteriously staying away from his room —"

The sergeant picked up his hat. "Let's go. You're one up on me, Phantom. I never gave that angle a thought. I'm assigned to the case, so if you don't mind, I'll go along."

They went first to the best hotel in town without getting any results. The second hotel, just as modern and expensive, was in a state of excitement when they entered the lobby. Night elevator operators, a couple of bellhops, and the desk clerk were in a serious huddle when the sergeant stepped up to the desk.

"Mathers," he said. "Identification Division. I want to know —"

"How many cops does it take to investigate a plain ordinary stickup?" the desk clerk said quickly. "I told the other men who were here that those bandits wore gloves and wouldn't have left any fingerprints. Identification Division, indeed."

The Phantom gave Sergeant Mathers a sharp glance.

"These safety deposit boxes," he said quickly. "Have you

notified the people who rented them?"

"Of course. The police wanted a list — and to know the contents, though of course that wasn't possible, with the envelopes sealed. So the guests had to be found, to tell what they had lost, all except one guest who hasn't returned yet."

"That's it!" Sergeant Mathers cried.

"I think so, too," the Phantom agreed. "We'd better have a look at the room that missing guest occupied."

A check revealed that the guest had registered under the name of Gerald Oliver and had given his home address simply as New York City. He had received no phone calls, made none, and no mail had come for him. The Phantom quickly described the height, weight and general appearance of the man found at the foot of the tower. The desk clerk and the others agreed the description fairly well fitted the missing guest.

The Phantom and the police officer were given a pass key and went straight to Gerald Oliver's room on the ninth floor. Two suitcases were at the foot of the bed, both closed. Mathers quickly opened them. They were empty. The Phantom was investigating the clothes closet. That, too, was empty. In the bathroom, there wasn't even a tube of toothpaste on the shelf.

"This is our man," the Phantom said. "The room has been searched and all his possessions removed. If they killed him, they'd have taken his hotel key and used it to get in."

"What about the stickup in the lobby?" Mathers asked. "That's just a little too coincidental to just happen now. This guy's safety deposit box was one of those burglarized."

"They knew about that, too, of course," the Phantom said. "It was impossible for them to get at the contents of that box without holding up the hotel, so they made it look like a straight stickup job with the boxes opened at random. . . . Well, this room needs a complete going over, but first let's have a better look at the suitcases."

"I wonder why they left them?" Mathers asked.

The Phantom shrugged. "Perhaps they intended to come back and plant some clothing in them which couldn't possibly be traced."

He checked through the first bag carefully, particularly making sure it wasn't initialed. There was nothing. In investigating the various flaps and pockets of the second bag his inquisitive fingers found a small square of cardboard. He gave a sharp whistle which quickly brought Sergeant Mathers to his side.

"Look at this," the Phantom said. "A baggage check from the Hotel Wayne in New York City, He must have checked this bag there at some time and when he yanked off the check, just dropped it into that pocket of the suitcase. This check happens to be numbered and porters in hotels as efficiently run as the Wayne will keep a record. I'm going to find out."

The Phantom went over to the telephone, put through a call, and in a few moments had a night porter at the Hotel Wayne on the wire. He explained what he wanted and held on.

"If this fizzles, we're really up against it," he told Mathers. "So keep hoping."

"I'm praying," Mathers said fervently.

The porter came back on the wire and the Phantom made some notes. When he hung up, there was a satisfied look on his face.

"That suitcase," he said, "was checked into the baggage room of the Hotel Wayne less than a month ago. By a regular guest who maintains a suite there on an annual basis. A man named George Lang."

"Never heard of him," Mathers said. "But we've sure got something to go on now."

The Phantom got up. "I'm leaving for New York on the next plane, Sergeant," he said.

Suddenly he sprinted toward the door, yanked it open, and was in time to see someone duck down the fire stairway. The Phantom yelled for Mathers to phone the lobby and have anyone stopped and to get there himself by the elevator.

"I saw the shadow of his feet under the door!" he called as he headed for the fire stairway himself. "He got an earful, and we must stop him if we can!"

But a search of the hotel and the entire neighborhood showed no trace of the man. The Phantom got into his car with Sergeant Mathers.

"Whoever he was," he said as he let in the clutch, "he could have been registered at the hotel and simply hurried back to his own room. We can't check everyone there, but somebody knows about the lead we've got. Which means I'll have to reach New York in time to stop that somebody from destroying any more evidence! I'm going to the airport now. You can take care of this car for me until I get back.

New York was still in the grip of early morning quiet when the Phantom taxied from the airport to the Hotel Wayne. There he identified himself to the night manager who was still on duty and to whom he gave a description of the man whose body had been found at the base of the TV tower.

"Yes," the manager said, "that sounds like it could have been George Lang. He has lived here for more than five years — in one of our better suites."

"When did he go away this last time?" the Phantom asked.

"It was at night, as I remember. Three — no, two days ago. Yes, that's when it was. He had two suitcases with him. A tan cowhide Gladstone and a regular suitcase. I think they were a matched set."

The Phantom nodded. That described the two bags he had found in the room of Gerald Oliver, the man who had checked into a hotel in Uncas and vanished. He was certain now that the dead man had been identified. But complete proof of that should not be so hard to get.

"Can you tell me anything about Mr. Lang?" the Phantom, asked.

The night manager hedged. "Well, frankly, we're not supposed to talk about our guests," he demurred.

"He's dead — murdered," the Phantom said curtly. "We're trying to find out who killed him and why."

"That's different," the hotel man said hastily. "Yes, I do know quite a lot about Mr. Lang. He wasn't a bad sort, although when he tried to lease a suite in this hotel five years ago, he almost didn't get it. And not because renting conditions were tight either."

"He wasn't — shall we say — a desirable tenant?" the Phantom guessed.

"That's right. He'd been in trouble a couple of times. I think he used to be in the black market during the war. Whatever he did, he had a lot of money."

"I see." The Phantom nodded. "Did he keep a hotel safety deposit box?"

"Yes, sir — and used it often. He took some papers out of it just before he left on this last trip. That's how I remember so well."

"What kind of papers?" the Phantom asked quickly.

"I don't know. He was careful that nobody could see exactly what was in the box, but I did see the general shape of them. There were maybe a dozen, folded. They looked like bonds to me."

"Look," the Phantom said. "Seal up that lock-box right away. The police are going to take over and you'll protect yourself by sealing it up in my presence."

The night manager gulped, then admitted: "I guess that's a pretty good idea, at that."

"Just a couple of more things," the Phantom said, stopping him as he was turning away. "Was Lang married?"

"No, sir. He didn't have any relatives at all I ever heard about."

"What of visitors? Phone calls?"

"We can give you a list of calls he was charged for. The last couple of months anyway. As for visitors, he had a few. Nobody I knew, and none of them ever sent up their names."

"Suppose I have a look at the phone call records," the Phantom suggested, "while you seal up that lock-box."

The records were promptly placed before him and the Phantom went through the score of printed slips which indicated the time, the number called and the charges. One slip was made out to a number in Uncas, the city where Lang had been murdered. The Phantom noted down that number and the date, which showed the call had been made the day before Lang left this hotel.

The Phantom then telephoned Inspector Gregory, a long-time friend, at Police Headquarters and recounted, briefly, all that had happened. Gregory promised to make a complete check on George Lang.

CHAPTER IX

THE PHANTOM'S TRAP

Quitting the telephone booth, the Phantom took a taxi and had the driver stop in a side street off Park Avenue, near the center of town. He dismissed the cab and walked briskly through the dawn to the rear of one of the elaborate apartment buildings. He entered it through a side door and a private elevator whisked him to his penthouse suite. He let himself in and, for the first time in hours, he relaxed.

He removed the light makeup he had worn during all that time, shaved and showered and put on a lounging robe over pajamas. When he looked in a full length mirror, the man who had been the Phantom in Uncas was gone. In his place stood tall, well-built Richard Curtis Van Loan, wealthy society playboy and sportsman.

Dropping into a chair near a picture window which overlooked the great city and one of its rivers, he dozed lightly. Now and then he stirred, to assemble his thoughts as he tried to reason out what lay behind that series of bizarre events into which he found himself merged.

He laid them out in his mind in sequence. To start the chain, an unknown man had been killed by a fall to a cement pavement. That could have been an accident except for one thing. The man was by no means a tramp as supposed, and yet he had been dressed like one. Either he had been in disguise, or someone had changed his clothing while he was unconscious. The body had been carried to the television tower — a risky business in itself. Someone had climbed the tower, carrying the corpse, and from a dizzy height had dropped the dead man to rocks below.

Next, an important man had hurriedly left town without even explaining his reasons to his daughter. A known gangster had moved in to the extent of dispatching hoodlums to beat up the Phantom, and later sent men to kill him in that old hospital.

The whole affair seemed based upon one thing. Someone intended that Alonzo Woodward's television station should be a failure, no matter what had to be done to sabotage it. The reason was obscure. The Phantom couldn't even guess what it might be, without any facts to back him up.

There was, of course, the idea of Brennan trying to muscle in. As Woodward had said, these days former gangsters were using all kinds of tricks to move into legitimate business where their evilly earned money could work honestly. Another idea concerned a man named Gordon Pulver who, apparently, had wanted to own and operate the most important television station in Uncas and had been beaten to it by Woodward. Those were motives, but neither one hardly strong enough to warrant murder and the risks such a crime involved.

Van Loan fell asleep in the middle of these thoughts and when he awoke, the early afternoon sun was shining in his eyes. He grunted in exasperation because of the time he had lost, then picked up his phone. He called Muriel Havens.

She was friendly as she always was when talking to Van, but there seemed something a little secretive about her voice, too. Van did manage to elicit the information from her that she had a visitor who would be staying with her indefinitely. Muriel was quite positive she couldn't go out — not even to an important polo match, or much advertised first night.

Van Loan grinned as he hung up. He put on a carefully tailored suit, selected a snappy hat, and picked up a pair of gloves on his way out. He took the house elevator this time, chatted with the elevator operator on the way down, and to a porter and a clerk in the lobby of the big apartment house.

He ate a quick lunch, then taxied to the offices of Frank Havens, where he was a well-known visitor. He was promptly admitted to Havens' private office.

"I really didn't expect to see you today, Dick," Havens said as he closed the door and snapped the lock. "What brought you back?"

Van Loan rapidly sketched in the developments for Havens who listened intently.

"I've heard of this George Lang," he finally said. "In fact, we probably have pictures of him in our morgue. I'll get you a photo before you leave. Perhaps, with the features of that dead man recreated, you might make a positive identification by using the photo."

"Thanks," Van said. "I'd be grateful for it, but perhaps Steve Huston ought to use it as an excuse for making a visit to that town. If you can spare him, he'd be handy to have around."

"You're going back soon then?" Havens asked.

"I've got to be there tonight," Van said. "Everyone expects fireworks. Woodward's television station has been sabotaged before, but tonight it joins a network, becomes a station of major importance and if those saboteurs intend to strike again, it will be tonight."

Havens pushed his swivel chair back until he was staring at the ceiling.

"Dick," he said, after a thoughtful moment, "the sabotage has already begun. It's no coincidence that one of the principal speakers on tonight's television program in Uncas has been warned to stay away or get hurt."

Van Loan showed his surprise and eagerness. "Then that may be the break I'm looking for, Mr. Havens! Who is the man and what are the circumstances?"

"He happens to be a foreign correspondent connected with my newspaper chain," Havens explained. "Man named Ben Corbett."

"Ah — yes," Van Loan said. "Wasn't he recently heaved out of one of the Iron Curtain countries?"

"That's right. And his speech on Woodward's new television station was to have been Corbett's first since his return — or I should say, will be. It's an important speech. Well, he's received three phone calls so far. The same man each time, with the same warning. To stay away from that broadcast or he'll get hurt. He's been told he'll be sorry if he goes to that city. But the threats have not deterred Corbett. He's an odd sort of person. Excellent reporter — honest as they come, but a bit of a prig. He thinks there's nobody quite like him, and basks in all this glory that's been coming his way since he was expelled by that foreign government."

Van leaned forward with interest. "Mr. Havens," he said, "I'd like to meet Corbett at once. Not here — preferably at his hotel. I have an idea."

Havens looked at him a little oddly, then nodded.

"Certainly I can arrange it," he said, with some asperity. "He works for me, doesn't he? I'll have him at his rooms in the Harrison House within an hour, waiting for you, Dick."

"Good," Van said. "And impress upon Muriel that Lisa McLean is still in danger, and that she must not go wandering around."

"What about Steve Huston?" Havens asked.

"Have him on the same plane which Corbett is going to take. Tell him to wait for instructions and I'll look him up in good time."

Havens arose and offered his hand. "Be careful, Dick," he said gravely. "Somehow I've got the idea there's something really big — and deadly — behind all this. There *must* be, to make McLean run for it. He never ran away from anything before in his life."

Van Loan nodded. "If you tune in on that new television show tonight, Mr. Havens, you might get an idea as to how things are going. My idea is that they'll try to wreck the program, though I wish I had even a glimmer of a notion why."

Havens shrugged. "That's simple enough, Dick. Somebody wants to take it over."

"But why wreck something you want?" Van asked. "If the premiere show on Woodward's new station is a flop, the business is going to lose a great deal of money. . . . Well, anyway, stand by your set. There should be fireworks."

Van Loan walked jauntily out of the office, greeted several old acquaintances among Havens' employees, and left the building. He drove straight back to his penthouse. Things were going to move fast from here on. He had a strong feeling about that.

In the privacy of his apartment once more, he changed back into the same clothing he had worn while in the city of Uncas. Then carefully he applied the same makeup until Richard Curtis Van Loan had vanished. He slipped two fresh guns into holsters, tucked a compact makeup kit into one pocket and a set of fine specially made delicate burglar tools in another.

It was the Phantom who turned toward the door, and he was now ready to set a trap. He needed bait for it, and he, himself, meant to be the lure which would draw those killers to him. Ben Corbett would have to cooperate whether he liked it or not. . . .

Ben Corbett was a man of only about forty-five, but he had gray hair, which he combed straight back. His complexion was florid, his face lean. There was a mole in the middle of his left cheek. An easily identifiable man.

He also proved to be as egotistical as Frank Havens had said he was.

"Of course I'm delighted to meet the Phantom," he said. "And naturally I told no one that you were coming here. When Mr. Havens phoned me he was quite insistent about that."

"He can be an insistent man," the Phantom assured, and grinned. "I need your help."

"If there is any way I can aid in running down that idiot who threatened me if I made my speech," the correspondent said, "I'll do anything you say."

"There is," the Phantom told him. "All I want is the suit you're wearing now. And your hat and shoes and credentials. I'll want your plane ticket also, and — your face."

"What?" Corbett exclaimed breathlessly.

"I mean it," the Phantom said. "Also, I'd like to have you make that speech right on schedule. But travel to Uncas by rail. You can get a train which will bring you there fifteen minutes before you go on the air. The television station isn't far from the railroad depot. You'll have plenty of time . . . And oh, yes — dress in a dark suit, wear dark glasses. Slip out of the hotel here without being seen and tell no one who you are. From the moment you leave here, until you reach the television station, you're simply nobody."

"But my face?" Corbett cried. "You said you wanted my face."

"Yes, I do. You'll see what I mean. Mr. Corbett, this is no reflection upon your personal courage. I doubt if you're afraid of these men who have threatened you, but if I take your place and they strike at me, I might be able to get a line on just who they are."

Corbett exhaled slowly and relaxed. "I understand now. You're clever at makeup, I've been told. You'll wear my clothes, and you'll look like me."

"That's it," the Phantom said. "Shall we get started? There isn't much time."

Corbett jumped up and began peeling off his coat. Within ten minutes the Phantom was in the newspaperman's clothes while Corbett had donned a more subdued suit. The Phantom sat down before the dresser mirror, placed his makeup kit on the dresser and went to work.

Changing his hair to gray and combing it straight back was a simple matter, as was the process of making his cheeks florid by the use of a cream which blended imperceptibly into his skin. The Phantom's own face was lean enough to pass, and he created a mole in the middle of his right cheek which was an exact duplicate of Corbett's.

A few strokes of an eyebrow brush and a fine line drawn at the corner of the eyes elongated them slightly. There were a few finishing touches, then the Phantom swung around.

Corbett, patiently waiting across the room, gave another startled exclamation. He came forward, his mouth agape.

"It's like looking into a mirror!" he marveled. "Phantom, I've never seen anything like it. You could pass for me anywhere."

The Phantom chuckled "You're the final judge of that, I think. Now suppose you start traveling. It will take you quite a bit longer than I, and by the time you arrive I should have things in hand. No matter what happens, go on with your speech. Don't let anything stop you."

Corbett bristled. "They've tried to stop me in a dozen different cities on this earth and nobody has succeeded yet. I'll make the speech, and I'll make it a humdinger."

Corbett put on dark glasses, pulled the brim of his hat down, then shook hands with the Phantom. "If I can be of any further help," he said, "call on me."

CHAPTER X

DEADLY DOUBLE

It was an hour before the Phantom left Corbett's room. Then he phoned for a bellboy, gave him the bag which Corbett had left packed, and followed the boy to the lobby. The Phantom walked over to the desk.

The clerk looked up, "Good afternoon, Mr. Corbett," he said. "You're not leaving us?"

"I'll be back tomorrow," the Phantom told him. "I'm not checking out. I have a television speech to make out of town. Hold any mail for me, please."

Casually drawing on his gloves as he turned around, the Phantom studied the people in the lobby with no apparent interest. No one there looked suspicious, but he had an idea he was being watched and wanted to make certain of it.

He walked over to a desk where there were telegraph blanks, wrote a message addressed to Alonzo Woodward, informing that he would arrive in plenty of time for the broadcast.

But before completing the message, the Phantom purposely misspelled a word, erased too hard and made a hole in the paper. He ripped the sheet off the pad and, with an exasperated gesture, threw it into the waste basket. Then he wrote another message, took it over to the telegraph clerk and asked to have it sent at once.

Nobody went near the waste basket. The Phantom asked the bellhop to call a cab. Strolling casually through the lobby, giving an excellent imitation of Corbett's egotistical manner, the Phantom passed through the revolving doors to the sidewalk, and headed for the taxi. He came to a sudden stop.

"Boy," he said, "put the bag in the cab and tell the driver to wait. I won't be a moment — and this is for you."

He scaled a coin at the bellhop, hurried down the sidewalk and turned the corner. In moments he had reached the side door to the lobby and through it he had an excellent view of the waste basket near the telegraph desk. A man was bending over it, hastily lifting out the crumpled papers at the top of the pile.

The Phantom waited until he had a good look at the man,

then he trotted back to where his cab waited. He told the driver to take him to the airport and settled back comfortably for the ride.

At the airport the Phantom stepped into a phone booth, faked a rather long call and smiled grimly when he spotted the man who had filched that telegram from the waste basket. The enemy meant to act, apparently, since Ben Corbett had refused to obey their demands. The Phantom looked forward to the meeting.

He climbed aboard the plane, and the man also had a reservation. Out of the corner of his eye the Phantom saw Steve Huston, the red-headed reporter whom Frank Havens had sent along to help. Huston wasn't a big young man, but he was husky and a fireball of action when it was called for.

The Phantom was assigned to a forward seat and as soon as the plane was airborne, he summoned the stewardess and protested his location. He didn't, he told her in no uncertain terms, like to ride forward. He stalked toward the rear of the plane, well behind the spy who had wangled a chair from which he could watch easily.

The Phantom sat down beside Huston.

"You don't mind?" he asked peremptorily.

"There's room for two," Huston grunted. "Sit down, Mr. Corbett."

"Oh, you know me, do you?" the Phantom asked sourly.

"I've seen your picture." Huston went back to reading his newspaper.

The Phantom had also provided himself with one and he opened it wide. Hiding behind this, he dropped his voice to a bare whisper. He spoke in a voice Steve Huston well knew — the voice of the Phantom, not that of Corbett, And as the reporter glanced up, the man beside him was thoughtfully pulling at an ear lobe.

"You're not very observing today, Steve," he said with a quiet chuckle.

Huston blinked rapidly.

"Holy smokes!" he gasped.

"So!" said the Phantom and grinned at him. "Now listen, Steve. In seat nine is a gentleman who has been dogging my steps. Watch him! And here are your instructions. When we land, I expect to be kidnapped. I'll be greatly disappointed if

I'm not. You keep your eyes open. It's arranged for a car to be waiting for you. Follow me and the boys who greet me. Got it?"

"Yes, sir,"' Huston replied.

"When you find out where they are taking me, stand by. Don't do anything until exactly ten minutes past nine. At a quarter after, the real Ben Corbett will step before the television cameras and make his scheduled speech. When that happens, I don't think the boys who have taken me prisoner are going to appreciate the joke."

"Got it," Huston said.

"If I don't come out at ten after nine, call the police and start something. Just let those boys know they aren't alone with me."

"Depend on me," Huston said grimly.

"I've found I always can," the Phantom told him. "Also take my guns now. Mind them for me. I hardly believe Corbett would be armed to make a television speech."

He passed the weapons to Huston who promptly tucked them away. Then the Phantom lowered his newspaper, closed his eyes and leaned back. He appeared to sleep for the rest of the brief trip. Huston just went on reading, wholly oblivious to the dozing man beside him.

The plane landed on schedule and the Phantom was one of the first to get off. He looked around, as if he expected someone to meet him. A man in a chauffeur's uniform walked up to him and touched the peak of his cap.

"Mr. Corbett?" he asked.

"Yes," the Phantom acknowledged. "Is Mr. Woodward here?"

"No, sir," the chauffeur replied. "He couldn't make it, but his secretary and a bodyguard are waiting in the car, sir. If you'll just follow me —"

"In a moment," the Phantom said. "I want some cigarettes and gum."

He took his time making the purchase, until he saw Steve Huston being guided by an attendant toward a parked car. Huston would be ready to follow now. The Phantom turned back to the chauffeur and walked to where a big, black sedan was waiting.

The chauffeur opened the door and the Phantom climbed in. He had to clamber over one man and sit down between him and another — a slim, well-dressed man. This man stuck out his hand.

"I'm Wilkins, Mr. Corbett. Mr. Woodward's secretary. We'll go to his suburban home for cocktails and a quick dinner before proceeding to the television station."

"Very well," the Phantom said. He looked at the other man beside him — a burly fellow — and at the back of the fat neck of another man who sat beside the driver. "Who are all these people?"

"Your bodyguards, sir," Wilkins replied promptly. "We heard you'd been threatened if you made the speech, so we took the liberty of taking precautionary measures."

"Bosh," the Phantom jeered, "Those threats were phony. They never worried me for a moment. Who cares if I make a speech? All this is unnecessary."

"Mr. Woodward doesn't think so," the man who called himself Wilkins said. "Anyway it won't be for long."

Once the car reached the city it threaded its way through traffic, kept on going clear to the other side of town. There they turned down a tarred road. The Phantom, having a fair chance to keep watching the rear view mirror, saw that Steve Huston's car had remained a respectable distance behind, but never lost the trail.

Then, as they turned into this less traveled road, a huge trailer van passed them from the opposite direction and started turning onto the main road. The driver seemed to miscalculate the distance and the big truck jolted to a halt, blocking the road.

That was the last the Phantom saw of Steve Huston's car. Of course that stalled trailer was part of a well-planned scheme. He was even more certain of it when the chauffeur made a turn onto another narrow road and headed back to another junction with the main highway.

They drove on through the advancing dusk until they reached a shabby old house set far back from the road. The Phantom let out an ejaculation of surprise when the car turned into the driveway.

"Is this where Mr. Woodward lives?" he asked incredulously.

Suddenly, without the slightest warning, the Phantom's arms were seized by the bulky man beside him. They were pinned behind his back and he was held helpless. He struggled a little until the slim man struck him a glancing blow on the chin.

"Stop that!" the man Wilkins warned. "Or I'll really conk you . . . Pete, roll up to the back door and then get those ropes. Snap it up."

"What's the meaning of this?" the Phantom demanded. "Woodward didn't send you!"

"Listen, my well-traveled friend," the slim man said, "What happens to you now depends on how much trouble you give us. You were told not to make a certain speech, but you wouldn't take good advice. Well — you're not going to make that speech. Got it now?"

The Phantom seemed to wilt. The car stopped and the driver leaped out, ran off into the gloom. When he returned, he was holding two thin, but tough pieces of cord. The Phantom was unceremoniously dumped out of the car. Before he could get to his feet, one of the big men flattened him to the ground again and held him there while the ropes were bound around his wrists and ankles.

They hoisted him up then, supported him between them and half-dragged, half-pushed him toward the back door of the house. Inside they shoved him into a chair.

The slim Wilkins straddled a straight backed chair he placed directly in front of the Phantom. He studied his prisoner for a moment.

"Did anybody follow you from the plane?" he asked.

"If they did, I never knew it," the Phantom said angrily. "Who's paying you to do this?"

"Don't ask questions, just answer them . . . Well, if you *were* trailed, whoever followed us got lost. That means nobody knows where you are, so it'll do you no good to holler. In fact, it'll draw you a fast punch on the jaw. Now make yourself as comfortable as possible. We all have quite a wait. One word out of you and we'll put you to sleep."

Wilkins got up, signaled the two burly men and they promptly took up positions beside the Phantom. It was dark by now, but no lights were turned on. Apparently the chauffeur and Wilkins parked themselves elsewhere in the house, watching all approaches.

The Phantom realized just what kind of a spot he was in. The precaution of having Huston follow was completely useless now. The truck had cut him off and he would never have been able to pick up the trail. And at nine-fifteen when these men would know their prisoner was a ringer for Ben Corbett, the fireworks would begin.

Cautiously the Phantom began work on the ropes. It was no use. They had been expertly applied and he was carefully watched. There was nothing to do but sit there and wait — and hope — and maybe pray a little.

CHAPTER XI

SKY-HIGH

Eight o'clock had struck somewhere when Wilkins came back from wherever he had been in the house. Using a flashlight sparingly, he went over to the corner of the room where the Phantom sat bound. There he snapped a switch and the viewing screen of a large television set lit up.

"Well, Mr. Corbett," Wilkins said, "I'll give you the pleasure of seeing who replaces you on Woodward's premiere program. Unless I'm wrong, he won't have anybody but the janitor to present to his audience."

The Phantom said nothing although he couldn't resist showing interest. In the half-light from the screen, he watched Wilkins fiddle with the dials and finally the test pattern of Woodward's television station flashed on. There was a fanfare of music. The test pattern faded to dark, then Alonzo Woodward stepped up before the cameras as they faded him on.

"Ladies and gentlemen," Woodward said, "what you are about to see this evening is the result of much work on the part of many. We have on our program such luminaries as —"

The voice was suddenly cut off. Woodward's lips still moved, but not a sound came out of the speaker. Wilkins suddenly began to laugh and he was joined by the two burly men beside the Phantom. Quite obviously the program had been sabotaged and while Woodward could be seen, he couldn't be heard.

The pantomime kept on for five minutes before an announcer stepped up to Woodward and whispered something in his ear. Woodward's more or less placid face developed hard lines. He signaled someone. The scene faded and was replaced by the test pattern.

Wilkins laughed harder than ever. When he finally found his voice, he decided to let the Phantom in on the joke.

"Know what happened, Corbett? We had a plant in there. All he did was throw a little switch. One little switch and Woodward's voice got lost. Brother, for an opening speech that one sure was a fizzle."

"I don't understand this at all," the Phantom said.

"Nobody asked you to even try. Just stick around and see

what happens next. There's a senator due to speak — only he won't. Because right now his car is stalled fifty miles from the television station and ten miles from a telephone. Then there are a couple of famous actors who were going to put on a scene from their new play. It's a costume play, and you know what? Their costumes have disappeared. There's an acrobat, one of the best in the business. Cost Woodward two grand to get him here for a five-minute show. He does his work on a trapeze. And guess what! They can't find the trapeze. This is going to be one honey of a program."

"Yes," the Phantom said, "I can readily see that. I won't be there either."

"Not unless you're twins, chum," Wilkins gloated. "We got this sewed up."

Suddenly the screen came alive once more. Woodward, a thin film of perspiration visible on his face, once more faced the cameras and this time his voice came over.

"I apologize for the delay, ladies and gentlemen. There were technical difficulties. All of you know this is a new medium of entertainment, that many things can go wrong, but we have them straightened out now. Please stand by. I shall forego my welcoming speech due to time limits, but there will be no more interruptions."

The screen suddenly went dark and Wilkin's laughter rocked the room. He slapped his thighs and cavorted like a school boy winning a ball game single-handed. The two thugs joined in the laughter, but the Phantom sat there quietly, feeling some of the sting which must be hitting Woodward about now. This was real sabotage, cleverly handled and meant to discredit the station as much as possible. Part of the entire nation would be laughing at what seemed to be the puny efforts of a new station to get its program going.

Then the screen lit up once more. A pretty girl, standing before an orchestra, was already in the middle of a song. It came over well. Wilkins stopped laughing.

"Wait!" he said angrily. "Just wait until they announce you, Corbett. Or try to explain why you didn't show up. You were supposed to be the star of this show."

"If only I could understand what this is all about," the Phantom said in a plaintive voice.

"Well you won't, so forget it," Wilkins snapped. "Get set, Corbett. I think you're supposed to be on after the singer. I wonder what happened to Woodward. And take a look at the announcer in the background! He's got his fingers chewed down to the knuckles. Even the orchestra's jittery. Huh — wait! Before this is over, those musicians will wish they were back in some theatre pit."

The Phantom had no way of telling what time it was, except when the unseen clock in the hall struck, but he guessed it must now be fairly close to nine. In minutes — perhaps seconds — these men here would realize they had been tricked. What would happen then wasn't pleasant to think about.

The girl finished her song. The scene faded and another camera picked up what seemed to be a corner of an office. Backgrounded was a huge colored map of the world. On the desk was a nameplate reading:

BEN CORBETT

An announcer came into view.

"Ladies and gentlemen," he said, "we are happy to present a speaker of worldwide fame. A man who has been behind the Iron Curtain, who has seen and knows exactly what life is like there. Ladies and gentlemen . . . Mr. Ben Corbett!"

And the real Ben Corbett walked blithely before the cameras and began to speak.

Wilkins let out a howl "Turn on the lights! Did you hear me? Turn on the lights!"

One of the pair of hoodlums stumbled over furniture, but found a switch. The Phantom closed his eyes tightly at the glare. They were snapped open again by a hard blow across the face.

Wilkins was staring at him, hand upraised for another blow.

"Who are you?" he demanded. "Who — are — you?"

The Phantom tasted blood on his lips. "I don't know," he said. "He must be a fake."

"Fake, is he? Listen to him talk! That guy's no fake. You are! Okay — so start doing some talking yourself. We've been buncoed, but I'm going to find out who did it. You got one second to open your yap and what you say better be good."

The Phantom shook his head and braced himself for the blow he saw coming. It came — harder than before. Wilkins' rage was maniacal. He raved his questions and kept slapping the Phantom's face until it was beet-red.

When he got tired of that he snapped a command to one of the burly men. Two hands circled the Phantom's throat. Two thick thumbs began a steady pressure on his windpipe that grew and grew until he was almost ready to black out. But he *had* to retain consciousness. He had to know what was going on.

The real Ben Corbett's voice droned on and on, describing some of the horrors he had seen. The Phantom had horror enough of his own to face. Suddenly he hoisted himself out of the chair. With his wrists bound behind him and his ankles tied, he was still helpless, but at least he was doing something.

One of the thugs raised a big fist and smashed it down on top of the Phantom's head. He was badly dazed by the blow, but still retained his senses, and be saw a slim chance to put an end to this torture.

He groaned weakly, let his knees buckle and fell in an awkward heap on the floor.

"You idiot —" Wilkins yelled. "Did you have to

The Phantom braced himself for the blow (CHAP. XI)

knock him out? An unconscious man can't talk, and I've got to know what happened. Somebody slipped, and whoever it was, so help me, he's going to pay! Get some water. Wake this phony up. And don't knock him cold again."

One of the men trudged away to get the water. Somewhere a telephone clamored, Wilkins muttered under his breath and hurried off to answer it. The Phantom had only one guard now, but he might as well have been in the center of an army of enemies for all the good it did him.

He was still helpless.

He heard Wilkins answer the phone, heard him tell, bitterly, how he had been tricked, and then the slim hoodlum did a lot of listening. Finally he hung up and came back. The thug who had crowned the Phantom had returned with a pitcher of water which he hurled at his victim's face.

The Phantom only moaned and didn't move a muscle. Wilkins kicked him, more or less experimentally. The Phantom had all he could do to keep himself from emitting another groan.

"Never mind that," Wilkins said. "We got new orders. Put down the pitcher, you big sap. Then go get that package of TNT. We're going to stop that broadcast before it goes much further. Wait and see! Woodward's going to have another surprise. In half an hour we'll blow down his blasted tower."

"The stuff's in the cellar," the big man said. "I'll get it."

"And be careful of it," Wilkins warned. "That stuff doesn't take rough handling. Marty, go upstairs and get some of those old clothes we got stashed up there. Something that will fit this punk."

"Okay," the big man replied. "But what's the idea? We bringin' him along?"

"Sure." Wilkins laughed harshly. "We're going to give him a little ride. Two rides. The first one straight to the television tower. The second one, straight up! And when the stupid cops start checking, they'll find what's left of him. Just another bum is what they'll think."

The Phantom gave no indication that he heard any of this. He realized, though, that his life expectancy had dwindled to a matter of minutes now. They weren't far from the television tower. During the few moments before they reached it, somehow he had to get free, overpower these men and prevent them from setting off those explosives.

How that could be done was only a jumble of ideas, none of them much good so long as those ropes stayed on his wrists and ankles.

Wilkins bent over him. Through slitted eyes the Phantom saw that he held a short-bladed knife. Wilkins slashed through the ropes that held the Phantom's ankles. Then he started slitting at the wrist ropes. The Phantom's hopes went soaring. He still had a little strength left. Augmented by sheer desperation he might overcome Wilkins before either of the two bruisers returned.

Suddenly Wilkins stopped cutting. He bent closer and slapped the Phantom lightly. Then he straightened up, stepped back and with the toe of his shoe turned the Phantom so that he lay on his back. The same toe pushed his head to one side so that the jaw was exposed.

Wilkins drew back his foot and kicked the Phantom squarely on the jaw. It was a brutal kick, meant to insure unconsciousness. The Phantom's last thought before he blacked out was a vague wonder about what Steve Huston was doing. . . .

As a matter of fact, the red-headed reporter at that moment was having troubles of his own. When he had first left the airport, he had found the trail of that big black sedan easy to follow. He'd had to stay close behind it through city traffic, but there had been so many cars he had felt certain his wouldn't be especially noticed.

Leaving the city, he let more space separate him from the big car, but he never lost sight of it for a moment. Huston knew well enough how important his part of this job was. Without him, the Phantom might be in a trap from which he could not extricate himself.

Both cars had sailed along a main highway at a good clip. Suddenly the brake lights of the car ahead flashed and Huston instantly slapped on his own. The big car made a difficult turn down a narrow side road. Huston made up his mind to be even more careful now. On a road without traffic he was bound to be noticed, and he was glad of the oncoming darkness.

He stepped on the gas until he saw the nose of that huge trailer truck emerge from the narrow road, make too wide a turn, then stall so that Huston was completely blocked. He stopped his car, reached for the door handle to get out and tell the truck driver to get that thing out of the way fast.

Then Huston hesitated. No experienced truck driver — and only an experienced one would have been allowed to handle such a monster — would have made so careless a turn. That had been deliberate. A move to stop any possibility of pursuit. If he showed his hand, let that driver realize he was trailing the big car, something abrupt might happen to one Steve Huston. The red-headed reporter sat quietly waiting.

The truck driver climbed out of the cab and Huston saw that he was alone. He stood at the front of the truck, showed his cap to the back of his head and scratched energetically as if sorely puzzled.

Finally Huston had to do something. He got out and walked casually over to the driver.

"Hey," he said, "you better get that thing out of the way before a trooper car comes along and hands you a ticket."

"Yeah," the driver grunted. "I'm tryin' to figure it out. Maybe if I back up a little, that will do the trick."

"Try it," Huston urged. "I'll yell signals."

CHAPTER XII

TALK OR DIE

THE PHANTOM DETECTIVE

Setting back into the cab of the truck, the driver started the motor and moved the big vehicle back a little. He jockeyed to and fro for a few minutes, and then with what seemed to be a mighty heave of the wheel, he managed to pull the rear end of it out of the side road and straighten the thing.

Huston's eyes were narrowed now. That driver knew his stuff, and knew it well. The redhead knew now that what this man had done had been deliberate, and that meant the driver had been hired to pull the trick. By now the car in which the Phantom was riding, was out of sight, and it would be impossible to pick up its trail. But Huston had ideas.

"Hey, driver!" he called. "Hey! The coupling pin came loose. It's barely holding."

The driver climbed down from the cab and walked over to where Huston was standing. He had bent to peer at the coupling pin when Huston grabbed him by the collar. With a terrific yank, the reporter lifted the fellow off his feet and sent him catapulting down the bank beside the road.

As the driver started to get up, Huston came racing down at him. Taking a long leap, the redhead landed on top of the man, knocking him flat again. He delivered half a dozen chopping blows to the back of the driver's neck, half-stunning him. Huston got up, hardly panting from his exertions.

Suddenly the driver's two arms flew out. Huston moved aside like an adagio dancer. The driver's hands clawed at air. Then Huston went into battle again. He aimed a punch at the big man's jaw, but it missed and only slid off the heavy jowl. The driver swept in a roundhouse. Huston tried to duck it but failed, and the blow caught him near the base of the neck. The power behind it bowled him completely over.

He fell, but was in full possession of his wits and managed to turn over fast before the truck driver came surging at him in a dive. Huston raised his legs and as the driver threw himself down, the reporter kicked out. His feet hit the driver's stomach. Huston felt the force of that kick all through his own body.

The truck driver flung his arms out, staggered back half a dozen steps toward the edge of another fairly steep bank. He lost his balance, fell, and rolled over and over, all the wind knocked out of him.

Before he could get to his feet, Huston charged halfway down the bank and threw himself in another long leap. Again he landed squarely on top of the man, delivering two short, chopping blows to the chin. This time the truck driver went limp.

Huston grabbed him by the collar and dragged him over to a tree. He propped the man against the trunk and searched him. He found a wallet and checked through its contents, then threw the wallet on the ground. Vigorously he slapped the truck driver back to consciousness.

Huston sat down, cross-legged, about four feet away and directly in front of the driver. There was a gun in Huston's fist pointed straight at the truck driver's chest.

"Hey, point that thing in some other direction!" the driver implored. "If this is a stickup, you can have my dough."

"We," Huston said stonily, "are about to have a little understanding. You don't own a truck driver's license. You deliberately swung that Goliath of yours so I wouldn't be able to follow a certain car down that side road. You were parked and waiting to do exactly that in case the car was being tailed."

"I don't know what you're talking about," the truck driver growled.

"You will," Huston promised. "It happens that your pals in that car snatched a friend of mine. They probably mean to kill him."

"It's still a riddle to me." The truck driver tried to sound complacent.

"Keep quiet," Huston snapped. "And just listen. Understand this, first of all. I'm not a cop. I'm not bound by any rule book. I'm just a guy with a loaded gun, and with a rat facing its muzzle, and I've got a strong yen to let you have it."

"But you can't!" The truck driver was showing alarm now. "Honest, I don't know what this is all about."

"If you don't, it'll be your hard luck. However, I think you do. I'm going to ask you one question — just once. If you answer it truthfully, you get a break. If you lie or deny you know the answer, I'll kill you. Where was that car you protected heading for?"

The truck driver moistened his lips, opened his mouth to make a denial, and closed it with a snap when the automatic in Huston's fist rose to dead center. Finally the big man shrugged.

"A guy named Wilkins paid me to block off the road," he growled. "I don't know who he is, where he went, or who was in that car."

The gun in Huston's hand exploded. Bark from the tree trunk flew with considerable force and made bloody streaks on the truck driver's face.

"Don't!" he howled. "Don't shoot again! I'm trying to answer. Give me a chance!"

"I purposely missed that time," Huston said. "Next time I won't."

"They had some guy they wanted to keep on ice for a while. Nobody said anything about killing him. I wouldn't get myself mixed up in no murder rap."

"If he dies, you will be," Huston observed. "And I'll see that you burn for it — if there's anything left of you to fry. Keep talking. I want all you know."

"They — took him to a house six or eight miles down the main highway. They used the side road as a cut-off in case they were followed, but it leads right back onto the highway again."

"Tell me exactly where that house is located," Huston demanded. "And you'd better know."

The driver talked fast enough now.

"On the truck speedometer it's exactly a mile and a quarter past an RFD mailbox with the name of Johnson on it," he said promptly. "They made me swipe the truck and stash it on the farm back of the house. That's all I know. Honest, I can't tell you another thing!"

"Are you local talent?" Huston asked.

"Yeah. Wilkins hired me in a barroom. I only swept out the joint, but I know something about cars. He didn't tell me it would be a snatch."

"Get up!" Huston arose himself.

"You ain't — ain't going to — to shoot me?" the truck driver asked nervously.

"Not quite yet," Huston assured him. "Walk ahead of me,

and walk slowly. I'm going to stow you away in the back of the trailer and drive it myself. We'll head for that farm. If the man I want is there, you can run for it. If he isn't, and you've lied, I'll probably kill you."

"It's the truth!" the driver mumbled. I ain't lyin'."

Huston shepherded him to the rear of the van, made him open the big doors and climb into the empty vehicle. Then he slammed the doors and snapped the lock on them. It was a pretty big cell, but about as strong as anything the county might have to offer.

Huston didn't know much about trucks, but he got this one going, found an open field, and turned the thing around. There seemed to be several gear shifts and he wasn't certain which one he was in, but the truck rolled fast and smoothly and he didn't care.

At least he knew where the Phantom had been taken, but it might be too late to do much about rescuing him. The clock on the dashboard of the truck read nine-twenty. The real Ben Corbett had been speaking on television for at least twenty minutes now. The Phantom's kidnapers must know the truth.

Huston set his jaw grimly. If they had killed the Phantom, there was going to be a bloody accounting. Maybe he wasn't the unerring marksman the Phantom was, but if the Phantom was dead, then a dead man's guns were going to talk, and Huston was not going to miss. . . .

Ahead, in the house where the Phantom was being held prisoner, he had regained his senses enough to realize, vaguely, that he was being searched. He was dimly aware that there were men around him who kept muttering, and the sound annoyed him. He wanted nothing but a lot of quiet until the hammer inside his head stopped beating his brains out.

There was another sensation then, after several minutes. It was like being in a hammock and swinging back and forth, except that sometimes he seemed to be jarred from head to foot. The air became cooler and fresher. It helped to erase some of the cobwebs in his brain. He half-opened his eyes, and restrained a groan only by using the utmost will power.

They were carrying him. One man had his arms, the other his legs and they were moving toward the same big car which had brought him here. Then it began to come back to him. The television program which had been so badly sabotaged.

The slaps and punches. The talk about blowing up the tower and him with it. Then that last kick delivered by Wilkins.

The Phantom wondered how much time had elapsed since that kick. Then he had no further time to think. They hoisted him up a little, squeezed him through the car door and onto the floor. He was doubled up uncomfortably and one hand was pressing against his neck.

He suddenly realized that the ropes had been removed from his wrists and ankles, and managed to get a glimpse of his left coat sleeve. It was a greasy old garment. They had taken away his own clothes and put some on him which would be impossible to identify.

An oblong package was shoved up against him. A man got in and moved the Phantom out of the way with his feet. Another man climbed in. Car doors slammed, the motor started, and they were beginning a trip which could well be the Phantom's last.

"How is that guy?" Wilkins said.

One of the burly men put the toe of his shoe under the Phantom's chin and pushed his head up and back.

"He's sure out. When that stuff goes off, this guy won't even know it."

"I wish I knew who he is," Wilkins muttered. "But we haven't got time to work him over. They got that program going somehow and we've got to stop it."

The big bruiser laughed. "Yeah, and pulling down the tower with a load of TNT is one way that works."

Wilkins bent down a little. The interior of the car was gloomy so he took a flashlight from his pocket, held it close to the Phantom's eyes and snapped it on. The Phantom knew what was coming, had braced himself for it and never moved a muscle, although the light hurt his eyes.

"He's out all right," Wilkins commented. "Just the same, we got a fifteen-minute ride, so put a gun on him. And watch him. This guy could be the Phantom for all we know."

"Yeah." The big man hoisted himself to one side and drew a nickel-plated revolver from his pocket. "The Phantom was pokin' his nose around plenty . . . Say, I heard he knows how to change his looks when he wants to. Maybe he's got stuff on his face now so he'll look like that Corbett reporter."

"If he has, it's a mighty good job," Wilkins said sourly. "I looked him over. But if he is the Phantom, we take no chances. He's a slippery customer."

The car made the turn into the highway and picked up speed. The Phantom rolled inertly as the car made turns, jogged up and down as it rode over bumpy roads. But all the while his brain was clearing and strength was flowing back into his muscles.

CHAPTER XIII

BULLET TO OBLIVION

Pushed up against the Phantom was a package which he knew contained high explosives. They were going to use it to kill him, unless he could figure out some way to make that TNT work for his side. There wasn't much time. He no longer expected any help. Steve Huston had been cut off and was probably wandering aimlessly over the countryside trying to find that black sedan. Whatever was to be done, the Phantom had to handle it alone.

He opened his eyes a trifle. Wilkins was at ease, looking out onto the countryside which whizzed past. The Phantom guessed they would reach the side road leading to the tower within a moment or two. If he was going to act, it would have to be now.

He gave a loud groan and moved his body. His right hand reached up and clawed at the car seat. Instantly the burly man with the gun bent down, shoving the weapon closer.

The Phantom's hand slid off the edge of the seat and moved fast. Fingers fastened around the thug's gun hand. The crook's finger, against the trigger, was suddenly pressed harder so that the hammer of the revolver was half-cocked.

"What's going on?" Wilkins shouted.

"Don't move," the Phantom warned. "This gun is pointed at that package of TNT. Your man can't let go of the gun and can't stop squeezing the trigger. If the gun goes off, we take the ride you've been talking about. Straight up!"

Wilkins started to reach toward his armpit. The Phantom applied a little more pressure. The gun hammer went back further.

"Don't try it!" the Phantom said. "You couldn't kill me fast enough to stop me from making this man pull the trigger."

"He's right!" the burly crook choked, "He's got my hand paralyzed. I can't help myself and if I try to yank free, the gun'll go off. Take it easy! I don't want to be blown sky high."

"Stop the car!" Wilkins yelled. "We'll see what weakens first. Your grip — or your nerves."

The car slid over to the curb and came to a dead stop. Wilkins leaned back again. "You can't hang on forever, my friend," he said. "And frankly, I don't think you'll pull the trigger unless you're forced to. Nobody wants to die."

"Get out of the car," the Phantom ordered. "Open the door and get out. Tell the two men in the front seat to do the same."

Wilkins shrugged. He bent forward and studied the situation. For the first time he saw the cocked gun and his eyes widened fearfully. He shouted an order to the men in. the front and all three got out of the car quickly.

The burly man, whose wrist the Phantom held in a vice-like grip, was groaning with pain.

"Boss," he pleaded, "I can't take this much longer. He keeps squeezing my wrist and pulling on my trigger finger. The gun's ready to go off! Anything will set it off!"

Still crouched on the floor of the car, the Phantom realized that headlights were sweeping down at him. Then he heard the rumble of an approaching van — a big one by the sound of it. Wilkins saw it coming, too. Suddenly Wilkins let out a yell.

"That truck — it's Joe! He's gone crazy. He's going to run us down. The whole business will blow up!"

Wilkins wheeled and headed for the brush beside the road. The driver and the thug who had been sitting in front raced after him. The Phantom was alone with the gunman, but he was getting worried, too. The sound of the truck was very close.

Suddenly the headlights veered off, air brakes hissed, and the truck came to a stop. He heard the cab door open and someone jumped down. The Phantom never relaxed his hold on the gunman's hand.

"If that's another friend of yours," he said, "you'd better explain fast what this is all about. I'm getting tired, too, but I'll blow all of us up before I'll let you kill me."

"Phantom!" a voice shouted, and the Phantom gave a welcoming cry.

Steve Huston ran toward them!

"Steve!" the Phantom called. "Watch for men hidden in the brush. Put a gun against the head of this one I'm holding. . . . Yes — that's it . . . Now I'm letting go of your hand, my friend. As I do, the gun hammer is going to fall slowly. When it's all the way down, drop the gun. Understand?"

"You win," the thug moaned.

Moving swiftly then, the Phantom was behind the wheel of the car while Steve sat in back with the thug. The Phantom tramped hard on the gas and kept up this high speed until they reached the vicinity of the television tower. There he stopped and got out. He opened the rear door.

"All right, Steve," he said. "Hand me my guns and I'll take care of our friend. You go across the street to that house which is lit up and call Police Headquarters. Have them send a well-armed detail to guard this tower. Those men who escaped may know where to get their hands on more explosives."

Huston nodded, handed over the guns and hurried away. The Phantom got in the back of the car with the gunman. He moved the package on the floor with his foot.

"That really is TNT?" he asked.

"Yeah, it's the stuff all right. Go easy with it, will you?"

"Which would you rather do — twenty years on a kidnapping charge, or four or five on a charge of conspiracy to destroy property?"

The thug sighed deeply. "What do *you* think?"

"If you tell me the truth, I won't press a charge of kidnapping. If you refuse, or lie, I'll see that you get the limit. I expect you've got a nice long record and when you get through squaring your accounts with the law, there won't be much of your life left."

The thug nodded heavily. "*Are* you the Phantom?" he asked. "Like that guy was calling you? Was Wilkins guessing about that?"

"He was," the Phantom replied.

"Okay. You're supposed to be a square shooter. I'll talk. I was hired to handle any rough work. The idea was to see that this television station wasn't going to open. Or if it did, to close it fast."

"Why?" the Phantom asked.

"I don't know. Wilkins is the only big shot I know and he didn't tell us much, but he paid off heavy. The way I got the idea, Wilkins works for a guy who wants the station for himself and figures on making so much trouble the guy that owns it will be glad to sell out."

"Where did George Lang fit into this?" the Phantom asked suddenly.

"Who? Lang? Honest, I never heard of the guy."

"All right. Then who paid Wilkins?"

"I don't know. Only once Wilkins said the guy who wanted the station should have had it in the first place."

"But he mentioned no names?"

"I swear he didn't. Wilkins is plenty cagey. I don't know

exactly who *he* is. He sent for us through a pal of ours. If I thought there was going to be killing mixed up in it, I'd have refused to go along."

"Um — I can imagine," the Phantom said. "Well, I'm going to check everything you've told me. All of it had better be right, and while you're locked up, do some more thinking. There might be a few items you — shall we say — forgot."

Steve Huston returned quickly and soon two police cars pulled up. The Phantom turned the thug over to them and also the package of explosives. Then he drove the big car a couple of miles away, parked it, and got in the back seat. He took his makeup kit from the secret pocket the hoodlums had overlooked. Steve, in the front seat, obediently looked straight ahead.

In minutes, the Phantom had changed his disguise from that of Ben Corbett to the one he had been using in this town prior to his New York trip. He grinned at the clothes he wore.

"Luckily," he said to the redhead, "I have an extra suit in my hotel room. And Steve, I didn't have time to say it before, but thanks for your help. You came along just in time."

"Just too late, you mean," Huston grumbled.

"No, because Wilkins and two other men weren't far away and they would have planned some trick to get me away from those explosives. They meant to kill me, Steve, and when you arrived, you scared them away. I'm not going to forget this."

"It was my fault you got into that mess," Huston observed wryly. "And say, that reminds me — I left the truck driver locked up in the trailer. We'd better send a police car out there to pick him up. He doesn't know much, but he did tell me where they'd taken you."

"Tell Sergeant Mathers," the Phantom advised. "He's working on this case and he'll do anything to help us. Right now we'd better get over to Woodward's television station and find out exactly what happened."

"The crooks fixed the broadcast then?" Huston asked.

"And plenty," the Phantom said. "I wonder what else they did beyond delaying actors, cutting sound switches and fading the whole show off the air. I'm afraid they didn't stop with that."

They found the television station guarded like a government mint. Huston's *Clarion* credentials and recognition of the Phantom as a man who had been working with the police, got them through the lines.

Sergeant Mathers was in Alonzo Woodward's private office. Woodward lay on a leather divan while a surgeon applied a bandage to his head. The station owner was moaning and apparently just coming out from a state of unconsciousness.

"What a business!" Mathers told the Phantom. "This station's enemies certainly wrecked tonight's show all right. Two acts never showed up at all. They cut cables and wires, threw switches, slashed scenery so much it was worthless. Two TV cameras were smashed — thirty thousand dollars gone there."

"I saw part of the performance," the Phantom said. "But what happened to Woodward? He was all right when he made his welcoming speech, even if nobody could hear what he said."

"By the time everything really started going wrong," Mathers explained, "Woodward went to this office and locked himself inside. That is, he locked the main door and forgot there was another leading to some of the studios. We found him tied and gagged. He had been whacked on the head until he was unconscious, and stuffed in that supply closet over there. We don't know exactly what did happen. He hasn't been able to talk yet."

"The show is still going on?" the Phantom asked.

"Yes — and okay, too. I brought along enough cops to guard every door and window. Whoever crowned Woodward must still be in the building, but unless Woodward can identify the man, or men, we're sunk. There must be at least a dozen spies planted here."

"I've been in a little trouble myself," the Phantom said, and went on to tell what had happened to him. He added, "This gang who kidnapped me was headed by a man named Wilkins. Slim fellow, about thirty-five. Fair complexion, brown hair and blue eyes. Well-dressed, a hundred and forty pounds, five-feet-seven. Ever hear of him?"

Mathers shook his head. "No, but I'll send out an alarm for him. I think whatever was done tonight was handled by out-of-town crooks. Some of them were planted right in the studio as scene shifters, engineers or clerical help. They certainly knew enough about the program to wreck it."

Woodward was trying to sit up while the doctor firmly

pushed him back on the divan. The Phantom went over and looked down at him.

"Are you able to talk?" he asked.

"I've got to talk." Woodward mumbled weakly. "Did you find the man in the shaft?"

"What shaft?" the Phantom asked quickly.

"One — of the men who — who hit me was going to do something to the power lines and cut off everything. He was in a hurry — ran to the elevator shaft. That door — behind you."

The Phantom turned his head. "I see it."

Woodward's voice strengthened. "He yanked the door open and stepped in. I know the car wasn't on this floor. I'd heard it going up a minute before they came in. I heard him scream as he fell. This is the third floor and the shaft goes down to a subbasement. He must be dead or badly hurt."

"Let's go!" Mathers shouted and the Phantom followed him out of the office to the stairway.

They raced down to the basement, opened the elevator door and Mathers threw the beam of his flash down to the bottom of the shaft. He let out a sharp whistle.

"Man, oh man!" he cried. "Woodward was right! There's a man down there and he certainly looks dead. How do we get down?"

CHAPTER XIV

THE SECOND CORPSE

Before long, Mathers found a ladder, and the Phantom climbed down it to the bottom of the pit to the body there. He felt for a pulse, found none, and turned the man over. He was a total stranger. When Sergeant Mathers joined the Phantom, he shook his head.

"I never saw him before, Phantom. Let's see what he's got in his pockets."

Mathers carefully searched the man, being careful not to move him too much. He found a gun in the hip pocket, a black-jack in a side coat pocket. There were brass knuckles and a fat wad of money in other pockets.

"Whoever he was," Mathers said, "he traveled well-heeled. With dough and weapons. I'll have him printed and see if there's anything in the records."

"Do that," the Phantom said. "I'll drop over to your office later to see what you find out about him. By the way, there's been no word from Chester McLean?"

"Uh-uh — not a word, Phantom. I don't like it at all. If McLean isn't dead, I can't help thinking that he could be boss-ing this whole affair by remote control."

"To force Woodward to sell his half of the TV station?" the Phantom asked.

"I've heard of worse motives," Mathers commented dryly.

"Yes, I agree. And McLean certainly vanished of his own accord, from what we've learned. So the chances are he is free to direct an operation like this from some hiding place. I won-der what Woodward thinks of the idea?"

"I think you ought to ask him," Mathers grunted. "After all, he's the guy who is going to be gypped."

"I'll talk to him, if he's able to talk at any length," the Phan-tom said. "You go to work on this dead man. There ought to be some kind of a record on a man who carries a gun, blackjack and brass knuckles."

The Phantom made his way back to Woodward's office. The owner of the station was feeling better, though still pale and nervous from his encounter with the men who had assaulted him.

"Did you find him?" Woodward asked as soon as the Phantom came into the office.

"We did, Mr. Woodward. He was killed in the fall. What about the others? Were there more than two of them?"

"I don't think so," Woodward replied. "It all happened so fast, I didn't even know they were in the office until I was struck a glancing blow with some sort of a weapon. I fell out of my chair and I saw two pairs of legs. Then I was hit again and while I didn't quite pass out, I was helpless. The blow seemed to paralyze me."

"I don't doubt it," the Phantom agreed. "We found the sap that was probably used on you ... Go ahead, Mr. Woodward."

"Well, there isn't much more. I heard one of them mention cutting the power lines and stopping everything in the station, I remember hearing him run toward the elevator and open the door. Then he screamed and — I guess that's all. When I woke up, somebody was dragging me out of the supply closet."

The Phantom sat down on the corner of Woodward's desk.

"They really broke up your premiere, Mr. Woodward," he declared. "It was partly done from inside, by men who undoubtedly work for you. Do you suspect anyone?"

"No," Woodward groaned. "No, of course I don't. But I hired a lot of extra people for this premiere. There wasn't much time to check on them, but they seemed okay."

"Have you heard from McLean?" the Phantom abruptly changed the subject.

"McLean?" Woodward asked in a surprised voice. "No, not a word. Have you?"

"No, and nobody else has either," the Phantom said. "Mr. Woodward, have you any idea why this is being done?"

"Certainly I have," Woodward replied. "Somebody either wants my station to fail or to drive me to such desperation that I'll sell out"

"Meaning Hugo Brennan, of course," the Phantom suggested.

"Well, he wants the station," Woodward said.

"What about this Gordon Pulver? I understand he wanted a big television station here in town, but you beat him to it, and you told me he's been sore about that ever since."

Woodward raised his bandaged head slowly and his eyes widened. "Pulver!" he exclaimed. "I haven't given him much thought. Listen, Phantom, I told you Pulver said I'd be sorry I cheated him out of the Federal license for this station. It wasn't cheating — I just moved faster than he did, that's all. But . . . Oh, no! Pulver's no crook. No killer. He wouldn't do anything like this."

"But he does have a motive," the Phantom reminded Woodward. "Revenge is one of the strongest motives for violence. I'm going to check on him. And on Hugo Brennan, too." The Phantom got off the corner of the desk. "About McLean again. He bought half of this station you said, didn't you?"

"Yes," Woodward admitted. "As I told you before I began on a small scale and thought I had enough to swing the deal. But when it got bigger than I anticipated, I had to have more capital. When McLean asked to buy in, I was glad to have him. He owns fifty percent of the stock."

"I see. If McLean is dead, his daughter will automatically inherit that stock, won't she?"

"So far as I know she will," Woodward said. "Nobody thought much about dying. We were too busy promoting this station. Phantom, if this keeps on, they'll wreck me! I can't take much more,"

"There's an inside man here — perhaps several of them," the Phantom said, "They'll be found. Meantime, be careful yourself. One way to stop the operation of this station in its tracks is by killing you."

"I'll be careful," Woodward said, and swore fervently. "I'm plenty scared too."

Sergeant Mathers bustled into the room.

"I'm going back to Headquarters with the dead man's prints," he said. "And there's something else. The boys from Headquarters told me that Brennan has been down there since fifteen minutes after the TV broadcast started. Seems he tuned in, saw what was happening, and beat it to Headquarters for an alibi. If he directed this business, it was all done beforehand."

"Thank you," the Phantom said. "That accounts for Brennan's movements, although he could have arranged the whole thing easily enough. I'm going to have a talk with Gordon Pulver."

The Phantom picked up Steve Huston, who had been prowling through the studios, and they headed for Gordon Pulver's suburban home. Huston had seen what those saboteurs had accomplished at the station and he was deadly serious now.

"They must have done forty or fifty thousand dollars' worth of damage," he told the Phantom. "They systematically wrecked everything vital for a business of this kind."

"And yet," the Phantom said musingly, "that program kept on going. It takes a lot to stop show business, Steve, and I know that now more than ever."

"Say, what about this Pulver fellow?" Huston asked. "Remember, I haven't been working with you long and I don't know all the details."

"Pulver, from what I can gather," the Phantom told him, "owned a small radio station here. But he wanted to set up a TV station and was preparing to do so, but Woodward filed with the Federal Communications Commission first. Until television becomes stronger, only one big station can survive here, and Woodward got it right from under Pulver's nose."

Huston whistled softly. "All of which didn't do Mr. Pulver's temper any good, I'll bet."

"They tell me he's a rather violent type," the Phantom commented. "But still, while he has a motive, he must know he is also an obvious suspect."

"Unless he's working with Hugo Brennan," Huston commented thoughtfully. "What brought Brennan to this particular town, wanting this particular station anyway? There are bigger stations he might have muscled his way into. Brennan's a big city guy, and while this town is no crossroads community, it hasn't got the flash of Chicago, Los Angeles, or New York."

"Maybe Brennan figured he'd have an easier time forcing his way into a smaller station," the Phantom argued. "But I've thought about Brennan being here on someone's invitation, and it could be Pulver's. We'll size up Pulver."

Huston glanced out of the window of the car in which they were riding.

"Say!" he discovered. "We're heading toward that TV tower."

"I know. Pulver lives a couple of miles beyond it, Steve. And this is the street where Chester McLean lives, too. His house is just ahead, and —"

The Phantom stopped talking so suddenly that Huston asked:

"What's wrong?"

"Nothing, Steve, except that I caught a glimpse of a couple of men across the street from McLean's home. It looks as if those crooks are keeping it under observation."

They passed the entrance to McLean's drive. Huston didn't turn his head, but he saw the two forms lurking in the darkness.

"Phantom," he said, "if the crooks are still trying to find McLean, then he certainly can't be mixed up in this business. He must have run away because he was afraid of Brennan."

"Perhaps. He was afraid of something. Don't forget, McLean was the first to call me in on this. He asked Mr. Havens for my help, but when I got here he lied to me and said he'd made a mistake. McLean is no coward, Steve. That much I'm sure of — and yet he ran out."

Huston wagged his head. "I wouldn't blame him for running from a man like Brennan."

"Steve, I doubt if he would run if his only reason was to protect himself. There's something else. I can't put my finger on it, but I'm betting that the reason for McLean's disappearance would go a long way toward solving this case."

Before Huston could comment on that, the headlights of the car flashed across a reflector sign bearing the name of Gordon Pulver. The Phantom turned into the driveway and stopped. He and Huston got out, walked up on the porch and Huston rang the bell.

The man who opened the door was tall, rangy, with sparse hair and cavernous cheeks. He had sharp black eyes, and his chin was thrust out belligerently.

"I'm a detective who is working on the television mix-up," his visitor said quietly. "And this is Steve Huston who works with me. We'd like to talk to you, Mr. Pulver."

"About what?" Pulver growled. "As if I didn't know. Come on in. I suppose it's easier talking to you than to the police."

Pulver's home wasn't as elaborate as McLean's, but it was comfortable and neat. Pulver had apparently been reading the newspapers, for they were in a disordered pile at the foot of a chair. Opposite that chair was an expensive television set, now dark. Pulver sat down, waved carelessly at other chairs, and glared at the Phantom.

"You're going to ask me if I had anything to do with that miserable broadcast tonight," he announced. "I saw it — all there was of it, and I'm glad it happened that way. I don't know who is behind this scheme to break up Woodward's premiere show, but I'd certainly like to shake the man's hand."

"I don't think you would," the Phantom said quietly. "Because that hand is getting itself bloodied with murder."

Pulver sat bolt upright, "Murder? You don't mean Woodward has been —"

"No. They beat him up some. One of the men who did was accidentally killed by a fall down an elevator shaft. I'm referring to the dead man who was found at the base of the television tower. He had been murdered."

"Good heavens!" Pulver exhaled slowly. "I had no idea —"

"Now you have," the Phantom told him. "Besides this, Chester McLean has vanished. He may also be dead."

CHAPTER XV

DEAD MAN FROM TEXAS

Unable, apparently, to take it all in at once, Pulver fell back in his chair. He moistened his lips.

Do you — think I've anything to do with all this?" he managed to ask the Phantom.

"I intend to find out," the Phantom said simply, "You did make threats when Woodward got the rights to that station away from you."

"Oh, I was just shooting off my mouth," Pulver hastily declared. "Anybody who knows me —"

"Some big-mouthed guys carry out their threats." Steve Huston said. "I've seen it happen."

Pulver leaned forward. "Look — I resented Woodward suddenly showing up with the permit for that station in the bag. Sure he put one over on me and I got sore. I thought about kicking his face in more than once, but I didn't. Because I'm a civilized man. I didn't think Woodward would go through with it, anyway."

"After he went to all the trouble of procuring the FCC license?" Huston asked.

"In my opinion," Pulver said, "Woodward didn't know much about broadcasting and had no idea of what it costs to build a TV station. He didn't have that kind of money. Frankly, I half expected him to come to me and ask me to buy in, but I guess I talked too much. He went to McLean instead."

"And then Woodward had enough money?" the Phantom queried.

"Apparently. He went ahead with his plans. Maybe he was shaky — I don't know. But he didn't have to worry. What he started out to make into a small local broadcasting unit got bigger. Then lightning struck, and the coaxial cable was unexpectedly branched out this way. Woodward's station became of major importance. He could get all the money he wanted after that."

"But a thing like this could wreck him, couldn't it," the Phantom wanted to know.

"Of course it could. Nobody can stand many nights like this one. I know what happened. I've got a few contacts inside Woodward's outfit, and they called me up. Let it happen a couple of more times and Woodward will go bust."

"And then you'd move in?" the Phantom asked quickly.

Pulver smiled widely. "Maybe — if I was certain I wouldn't be bothered this way. But don't accuse me of directing that sabotage. I had nothing to do with it."

"Do you know Hugo Brennan?" the Phantom asked.

"I know who he is, that's all. I've never talked to the man in my life. But if you go after Brennan, you're on the right track. Being in the radio broadcasting business, I follow the news closely. I know how ex-racketeers are trying to force their way into decent, established businesses. Why else is Brennan here? What is there in this town, outside of the TV station, to draw a man like him?"

"You could be right," the Phantom acknowledged. "But you'd better be careful, too. As a prime suspect, be sure to keep your skirts clean, Mr. Pulver. Thanks for telling us what you know."

He and Huston left the Pulver home and headed back to the city. The *Clarion* reporter was slumped way down in the seat, smoking a cigarette with long puffs.

"Phantom," he finally said, "did you notice how Pulver admitted he had spies planted in Woodward's outfit?"

"I did, Steve, and I know what you're thinking. It took inside men to handle the sabotage tonight. Pulver gave us a good story, but I've far from dropped him as a suspect. What's more, seeing those men watching McLean's house has given me an idea."

"If you want them grabbed," — Huston grinned — "I can do that. And I've become expert at making punks talk."

"No — those men will help us in my scheme," the Phantom said. "I want to be sure that somebody is as eager to find McLean as we are. Suppose I write a letter, apparently to Lisa McLean and sign it with her father's name. When it's delivered, those two stake-outs are going to find out what's inside the letter. I'll plant information which might bring Wilkins, or someone as important, to a spot where we can move in fast."

"That'll work," Huston said eagerly. "They'll be sure to bite on a thing like that."

"Then I'll arrange it as soon as we reach Police Headquarters. Nobody else will know anything about it, Steve, so don't make any slips. Whoever is behind this business might possibly have spies at Headquarters, too. You never can tell."

Sergeant Mathers was in the police lab when the Phantom and Huston arrived at Headquarters. Mathers looked a trifle smug as he laid a criminal file on the table before the Phantom.

"There," he said, "is the man who conked Woodward on the head, then fell down the elevator shaft."

"So I see." The Phantom studied the card. "His prints were on file, then. His name is Tom Finley. Last known address was San Antonio, Texas, and prior to that he was a guest at several state prisons. Most interesting, Sergeant. I also notice he is not listed as a wanted man. Had he reformed?"

Mathers chuckled. "Finley's got quite a history, Phantom. He didn't hit the East often, but in the Southwest he certainly raised hob with plenty of banks. That was his line — bank robbery. The authorities in San Antonio told me over the phone a few minutes ago that Finley was the kind of a burglar who could almost talk a safe door into opening for him."

"Go on," the Phantom urged. "I can tell by your face there's plenty more about Finley."

"Well, about two years ago a small town bank was hit one night. The burglar really hit pay dirt with that one. Some oil company had a pay-roll in the vault and the robber got it. Two hundred grand, Phantom, and all in nice spendable cash."

"Was Finley suspected of doing the job?" the Phantom asked.

"It had all the earmarks of his fine hand, Phantom. But they couldn't pin it on him. Yet they've become sure since then that he pulled the job because from that time, Finley's been retired."

"Nice work," the Phantom commented. "But I've got only one objection to it. If Finley was so well heeled, why should he join forces with the gang operating here?"

Mather's smile died. "The same idea struck me. But Finley really did pull in his horns — bought a little cottage, started raising chickens, and seemed to settle down. It looked as if he didn't want to stretch his luck any further,"

"So he comes up here, associates himself with a cheap mob," the Phantom commented. "Assaults Woodward and tumbles down an elevator shaft like some amateur operator. I don't go for it, Sergeant. How about you, Steve?"

"If I had a long record like that," Huston said, "had cleaned up two hundred grand and settled down, I'd stay settled. Besides, if Finley was a bank robber, how come he turned his talents to assault and battery? It won't add."

"Then what is your theory?" Mathers demanded. "I can't figure one. Can you?"

"Not right now," the Phantom admitted. "And we can't spend too much time on Finley. I've got a letter to write which may give us a lead. Then we'd all better get some rest. This hasn't been what you might call a quiet evening. . . ."

Shortly after nine o'clock the next morning, Steve Huston and the Phantom parked their car half a mile from the McLean home and approached the big house from the rear. Finding a thick clump of shrubbery which would conceal them well, they crouched down behind it.

From there they could see the front porch and the mail basket near the door. If the two men they had seen keeping watch on the place were still around, they stayed under cover. The Phantom however, had a good idea that the arrival of the mailman would bring them out of hiding.

Shortly before ten the mailman walked up the drive, onto the porch, and deposited a single letter in the basket. He moved off, and nothing happened for almost half an hour. Then the Phantom whispered a warning. Huston also spotted the man who flitted from behind a tree to a row of lilac bushes growing at the far end of the porch.

After a moment or two the man appeared again as he scaled the porch railing. Crouched, to stay out of sight as much as possible, he scurried to the mail basket, reached up and filched the letter. Then he retreated just as he had come.

"And that's that," Huston sighed, satisfied. "Now what?"

"In the letter," the Phantom said, "I wrote as I believe Chester McLean would have written to his daughter. I wrote that I was hiding at a certain hunting lodge ten miles from here, and that I was all right. I warned her to burn the letter and say nothing to anyone, and that soon I'd tell her to meet me and I'd explain everything."

"If that doesn't draw some action, nothing will," Huston declared. "Unless McLean is in on the deal, and they know the letter must be phony. When do we start for the hunting lodge?"

"Right now," the Phantom said. "They may move fast, and we want to be there."

The Phantom had selected this particular hunting lodge carefully. It was located halfway up a mountainside and in a clearing so that it could not be approached by stealth. As soon as he and Huston got there they selected a good spot where they could see everything.

"If they come gunning for McLean," Huston said, "I hope nobody else is in that lodge, Phantom."

"It's not occupied," the Phantom said. "Sergeant Mathers gave me the information on it. The owners are in Hawaii. Now, Steve, unless something happens that demands we move in, don't let them know we're here. All we do is stay hidden."

"With a chance like this?" Huston asked in a surprised voice. "If there aren't too many of them, we can take them."

"That's what we don't want to do," the Phantom declared. "We're after one particular man, Steve — the man who is behind all this, and he isn't likely to show himself. The men who do come can lead us to the killer we're after. That's the whole idea of this trick."

"Okay," Huston said. "If that's the way you want it."

"I do, Steve. These little fellows are dangerous, but they can be replaced. That is why we have to get the big man behind them. Just stopping him isn't enough. We want evidence to put him where he belongs."

"You know" — Huston found a comfortable spot and lay on his back to look up at the clear sky — "I've half an idea you know more than I do. You've got ideas and they make sense. All I can see is some guy trying to take over a valuable television station by intimidation, sabotage and maybe murder."

The Phantom kept his eyes glued on the approaches to the lodge as he answered. "There's more to it, Steve, but we must have proof. And, even more important, we're trying to save a man's life."

Huston sat up quickly. "McLean's?"

"That's right. Also the life of his daughter. I think McLean ran away because things were closing in on him, but I'm betting he was more afraid for Lisa than himself."

"But he left her behind," Huston protested. "That's no way to protect her."

"Perhaps it is," the Phantom said, with a grin. "Sometimes all we see is on the surface. We don't dig deep enough. In my opinion, McLean ran away because, if he vanished, Lisa would remain safe."

"Maybe you ought to draw me a picture," Huston grumbled. "I can't see any sense to it."

"Later, Steve. Right now let's keep our attention on this lodge. Something ought to happen soon. Wilkins isn't the type to lose any time and I'm sure he'll boss the raid."

But an hour went by before they heard the sound of a car motor grinding up the winding, steep road to the lodge. They lay flat, parting the brush just enough so they wouldn't miss anything.

The sound of the car stopped suddenly, and there was nothing but a lot of silence for a time. Then two men suddenly appeared from the forest surrounding the lodge. They were crouched and running. Each man held a gun in his hand. They dodged down below a window near the porch. One of them crept around to the steps, climbed them, and approached the door. The other man stood with his gun aimed, to cover his partner.

The man on the porch tried the door knob gently. The door was locked. He sidestepped to a window and peered through the glass. Finally he took a slim piece of metal from his pocket, worked this between the window frames and forced the catch back. He then signaled his companion, who quickly came up on the porch.

The window was raised slowly and carefully. One man climbed over the sill. A moment later he opened the front door and both men disappeared inside, obviously to make a search of the premises. Someone must have signaled the car driver because the motor started up again and in a moment the sedan appeared.

The Phantom spoke softly. "Steve, when they leave here, we'll cut down the back trail as fast as we can travel. We can reach the spot where our car is parked, before they can get that far. Then well —"

"Phantom," Huston interrupted in a strained voice. "Look! They've dragged a man out of that car. He's been beaten up! Is that McLean?"

"No," the Phantom said. "I never saw that man before. What is this? I never expected anything of this nature."

"The guy can hardly walk," Huston whispered. "By the looks of his face he must have been pistol-whipped!"

CHAPTER XVI

MYSTERIOUS PRISONER

Cautiously, but intently, the Phantom and Steve Huston watched the scene below them. Wilkins had come, as the Phantom had expected he would. He was approaching the lodge slowly with a drawn gun. Behind him standing beside the car, were two of his burly gorillas, supporting between them a fairly husky man who looked as if all the fight — and almost all the life — had been beaten out of him.

Wilkins stopped and looked over his shoulder.

"Okay, bring him along," he ordered. "They must have found McLean by now. We'll get this over with."

The two gorillas propelled their prisoner forward, over the pebbled driveway. The man stumbled, sagged in their grasp. He seemed to have passed out. One of the men lifted him, but in doing so he had to let go of the man, so that only his companion supported him.

Suddenly the prisoner brought up a fist. Where he summoned that strength was a mystery, but he banged the fist against the thug's jaw and sent him reeling backward. At the same time he wrenched free of the other man's grasp, started running for the brush. Both men were after him in a flash and Wilkins joined in the chase.

They were gaining, because the prisoner's surge of energy was short-lived. He had begun stumbling already. Suddenly he bent down, scooped something up from the high brush beside the driveway. It was a large soda pop bottle, and he swung it hard.

The man at whom he aimed it dodged quickly. Then they all piled on him. It was over in a few seconds. They used gun butts and when they had finished, their prisoner lay in an inert heap.

Huston nudged the Phantom. "We could take them, Phantom. And brother, wouldn't I like to!"

"So would I," the Phantom whispered, "but they were careful not to kill that man. If they had tried, I'd have opened fire on them. He'll have a better chance to stay alive if we trail these men."

The pair who had invaded the lodge hurried out. The Phantom couldn't hear what they said, but their gestures indicated that not only had they found the lodge empty, but there were no indications McLean had ever been there.

Wilkins suddenly looked around, and fear was written plain on his face. He gave quick orders. The prisoner was picked up and carried toward the car. Wilkins kept turning slowly, watching the whole area as if he expected an attack to develop any moment.

The Phantom and Huston were already running down a trail which formed a short cut to the highway back to town. They couldn't waste a moment now. They found their car as they had left it, backed off the highway and out of sight. The Phantom got behind the wheel. Huston waited beside the large, heavily foliaged branch which concealed the car.

In no more than thirty seconds, Wilkins' car flashed by, traveling at top speed. Huston promptly raised the branch. The Phantom drove out from beneath it, and Huston jumped in. Following the car in which Wilkins was riding was a difficult task in broad daylight, and required all of the Phantom's ingenuity. He never dared to get too close, and once he lost the car. But he picked up the trail a mile further on and when they reached the city limits it became a routine job of shadowing.

"Phantom," Steve asked, "who do you suppose that fellow is they've taken prisoner?"

"I don't know," the Phantom replied, "But I can guess why they brought him to that lodge where they thought McLean would be hiding."

"I wish you'd tell me," Huston sighed. "I can't figure it out."

"They were either going to have McLean kill this fellow or have the man kill McLean. Perhaps the survivor would then be killed by them, and the whole thing rigged to look like murder and suicide."

Huston nodded. "It must have been something like that or they wouldn't have risked bringing a desperate man all the way to the lodge. But I wonder why . . . Hey! Where's the car?"

The Phantom had turned a corner and on the street into which he headed only two cars were moving. Neither was the Wilkins car. The Phantom quickly pulled to the curb and stopped.

"They weren't far ahead of us," he said anxiously. "It was impossible for them to have reached the next corner and turned it before we drove into this street. They must have swung into some alley or driveway. We'll wait a few minutes to see if they come out again. If they don't, we'll start a building to building search for their car."

Five minutes went by and neither man spoke. Both were too worried. If Wilkins vanished, all their work would have been for nothing. Then Huston gave a warning grunt and the Phantom also saw the car that was pulling out of an alley.

They started up again. This time the chase was not a long one. It led to a nice part of the city and a street lined with high-class apartment houses. Wilkins got out of the car after it was parked at the curb, and he was followed by two men. They moved toward the entrance of the one of the apartment houses.

"Phantom," Huston said, "that beat-up guy isn't with them any more."

"So I see," the Phantom commented. "They must have dropped him off at that last stop. Look — you need a key to enter an apartment house like that and Wilkins has one. He probably lives there."

"He'll sure be easy to take now," Huston said hopefully.

"We're not ready for that yet, Steve. Wilkins is important to us, but not nearly as important as the man for whom he works. It's through Wilkins that we'll find out why Woodward's television station is being sabotaged and who is behind the scheme."

"What'll we do?" Huston asked. "Put a stake-out on the place?"

"Better than that. We'll have Sergeant Mathers put a wire tap on Wilkins' telephone. I'll take care of that. There's something else I want you to do."

"Just name it, Phantom," Huston said eagerly.

"Take this car and drive back to the hunting lodge we just left. Remember how the prisoner picked up some sort of bottle and tried to use it as a weapon? I want that bottle, Steve. And be careful of it, because what I'm after are the fingerprints of that prisoner."

The Phantom braked the car and got out. Huston slid over behind the wheel.

"I'll meet you at Sergeant Mather's office," he said. "Hope your wire tap works out all right. . . ."

It was early evening before the Phantom's plans were all set.

Then in the basement of the apartment building, where he had discovered Wilkins really did live, two of Sergeant Mathers' crack detectives were manning a wire tap.

Steve Huston had returned with the big soda pop bottle and it was being put through the Identification Division. Huston waited impatiently in Mathers' office. Shortly after seven o'clock the Phantom arrived. He sat down with a long sigh.

"Well, Phantom," Mathers said. "Wilkins hasn't made any calls yet. But he hasn't left his apartment either, and nobody's arrived or called him."

"He won't sit there long," the Phantom prophesied. "What about the TV show tonight?"

"It's coming over okay," Mathers said, "I'm having a receiving set monitored to keep check in case something else goes haywire. Woodward called a little while ago and said things were quiet. I've got a strong force of men guarding the tower."

"Good man, Sergeant. I've been busy myself. Tell me, what do you think of the integrity of Attorney Paul Miller?"

"First class," Mathers said promptly.

"Good enough. Miller happens to be McLean's lawyer and I have just paid him a little visit. I wanted to find out what happened to McLean's estate in the event he was killed. I found out. It all goes to his daughter Lisa."

"Do you think he's dead, Phantom?" Huston asked.

"No, I don't. But if he is, Lisa owns half of the TV station. She becomes a full partner with Woodward. If Lisa dies, her shares in the business will revert to Woodward. Just a good business arrangement. Woodward is protected against some remote heir moving in."

Sergeant Mathers drummed the surface of his desk with his fingertips.

"Phantom," he said slowly, "do you think Woodward might kill McLean and then kill Lisa to get full control of the TV station?"

"If that was all there was to this, I'd say Woodward had an excellent motive," the Phantom replied. "But why should he sabotage his own station? Practically wreck his premiere show and damage a great deal of property? Why should an out-of-town former black marketer be murdered?"

"I guess you're right," Mathers said. "Woodward has suffered the most in this business so far."

"But you did suspect him there, for a moment," the Phantom said. "Why, Sergeant?"

"I don't know. Just the natural suspicions of a cop, I guess. Woodward came here a total stranger. Nobody knows much about him. He speaks little of his former connections, but perhaps he doesn't like to boast. Anyway, he did our city a big favor in giving us an important television station."

One of Mathers' men came in with a report on the fingerprints found on the bottle. Mathers looked at the report and whistled sharply.

"Say, Phantom, I'd certainly like to catch up with the man who swung that bottle. He happens to be Hank Jobe. Ever hear of him?"

"No," the Phantom answered. "I don't think I have."

"About five years ago Hank Jobe was the cashier of a bank in Oregon. He liked living on a better scale than his salary provided so he helped himself to a hundred thousand of the bank's money and vanished. It was believed that he had adopted another identity and was living somewhere in California, but in five years nobody has ever run across him!"

The Phantom wrinkled his forehead. "Odd," he said, "Jobe seems to be slated for death, and if they kill him he'll be the third out-of-towner to die here, George Lang, an old-time black market operator from New York; Tom Finley, a bank robber from Texas; and now Jobe, an absconding bank cashier from Oregon and California."

"But Phantom," Huston objected, "you can't put Finley in a class with the other two. Finley is on the side of these local crooks. He died accidentally while he was trying to sabotage that TV show."

"All of those men are crooks," the Phantom said. "Who can tell what side they were on?"

Mathers snapped his fingers. "Listen! I've got an idea. Go ahead and laugh if you like, but it makes sense to me. Those three known crooks were after Woodward, maybe with a motive of revenge. That's what brought them all here. I can't explain why they were killed, or who killed them, but Finley certainly did his best to injure Woodward. We don't know about George Lang, the man we found at the base of the tower, but he was involved in some way."

"How about Jobe then?" the Phantom asked. "We're pretty sure that Wilkins is working against Woodward and the TV station, so he must be on the same side as Jobe. Yet he is holding Jobe a prisoner and treating him badly."

"I can't explain it," Mathers said, "but maybe Woodward can. I suggest we go see him right now. Perhaps when we name those three men, something will click in Woodward's mind. It's worth trying."

"All right," the Phantom agreed. "But you'd better let the desk officer know where we are in case something develops on the wire tap at Wilkins' place."

"I'll do that. Meet you at the car. I've got a hunch we're beginning to go places."

Mathers grabbed his hat.

CHAPTER XVII

FLAMING ATTACK

During the short ride to the TV station, Mathers continued to expound his theories, and he did present them as fair possibilities of a motive for murder and violence. But when they arrived, Woodward, who had them sent straight to his private office, showered the idea with cold water when Mathers told him the facts.

"George Lang, Tom Finley and Hank Jobe are total strangers to me," he said. "I never heard of either of them before. They seem to have come from widely separated parts of the nation, too, and while I've been in the cities which were their homes, I never came across them."

"You've traveled a lot then?" the Phantom asked.

"A lot?" Woodward laughed. "Phantom, I used to be a traveling salesman, I've been in every state, in practically every city and town of any size at all. I sold hardware."

Mathers was disgusted and showed it.

"I thought you'd settle this whole thing for us, Mr. Woodward, when I mentioned those men. Well, we've been on the wrong track again."

"But haven't you made any progress at all?" Woodward asked.

The Phantom answered that one.

"I think you ought to be told the truth, Mr. Woodward," he said. "We know who is actively directing this campaign of sabotage against you, but we don't know who is behind this man. However, there is every indication we soon will know."

"How can you be so certain?" Woodward asked. "Oh, I know I've no right to make demands, but after that beating I received last night, I can't help but worry. Who knows what will happen next?"

"Has anything happened so far tonight?" the Phantom queried.

"Not yet. But it's too quiet. They can't have given up. Why don't you arrest this man you just told me about? Force him to tell you who hired him."

"I'm sorry," the Phantom said. "But I know he wouldn't talk. We really haven't too much against him yet, anyway. But we have got his phone tapped and sooner or later he's going to call someone or receive a call. We'll get a lead from that, so you'll have to be patient."

Woodward spread his hands in a gesture of resignation. "All right. There is nothing I can do. However, I've been thinking about asking for protection."

"You'll get it." Mathers picked up the phone. "I'll put two men at your side every moment. The building here is well-manned already. You shouldn't have any more trouble."

"What about McLean?" Woodward asked. "Have you heard from him?"

"Not a word," the Phantom said. "But it's clear that he went away voluntarily. Tell me, is there any reason why he'd want to wreck your station?"

"None that I can think of," Woodward replied promptly. "We're partners, and his losses are as great as mine. But I *would* like to know what he ran away from, and why he didn't tell me he was going."

Mathers put down the phone after a brief conversation with Headquarters.

"We'll have men over here in ten minutes, Mr. Woodward," he assured. "They've got orders never to let you out of their sight."

"I'm grateful," Woodward said. "And let me know if there are any developments."

The Phantom hesitated for a moment. "Mr. Woodward," he asked then, "what about Gordon Pulver?"

"Pulver? Why I —" Woodward's eyes suddenly opened wide. "Phantom, have you any reason to suspect him?"

"Perhaps. Nothing definite, unless you can help us."

"Well, I think I've already told you that Pulver swore he'd own this TV station some day. He openly threatened me when I got the jump on him. It struck me then that he is a vindictive sort. Do you think it's possible that he's hired these thugs and crooks to break my station? To force me to spend so much money that I'll have to sell?"

"It's a good motive," the Phantom commented.

"It's the only one. Phantom, if Pulver is behind this, I can even guess why McLean has vanished. Pulver forced him to run away, probably under a threat of being murdered. Or Lisa may have been threatened. McLean wouldn't be here to lend his financial support when things went wrong. Pulver would only have one man to break — me!"

Mathers was all for the idea.

"Things are beginning to clear up," he exulted. "It all ties in."

"Yes," the Phantom said, "I admit that, but we still lack evidence, and locking Pulver up won't accomplish anything. In the first place he'll get out quickly and we'll have tipped our hand. So let's take things quietly and keep this a strict secret between ourselves."

"I agree," Woodward said. "With detectives at my side, I'll be protected. If Pulver is behind this, get him. But make certain you have enough to hang him!"

Huston drove the Phantom and Sergeant Mathers back to Police Headquarters. There wasn't much to do now except wait for Wilkins to start something. And by the time they returned, he had. The desk officer told Mathers that the men on the wire tap had called and he was to get in touch with them at once.

Mathers called from the phone in his private office and got the men in the basement of the apartment house where Wilkins lived.

"We just recorded a call, Sergeant," one of them reported, "and it sounds important. I'll play it back to you off the tape. Hold on a minute."

Mathers summoned the Phantom. "Get on that other phone. They're going to play back a call Wilkins just made."

The Phantom picked up the other phone. Suddenly he heard the dial click of a phone as a call was made. That could be translated into figures and traced. Then he heard a muffled voice speak a cryptic greeting. Wilkins came on next. There was no mistaking his voice.

"We're all set," Wilkins said. "The payoff is around nine-thirty. By then they'll figure nothing is going to happen at the station tonight. Our man has cooked up something that will wake them up fast — but too late. Much too late."

"Good!" the muffled voice exclaimed. "We've been wasting too much time. Get it over with."

"After tonight," Wilkins chortled, "the whole thing will be over. We can't miss."

Both phones clicked and the line went dead. Mathers and the Phantom hung up. There were beads of sweat on the detective sergeant's forehead.

"What kind of a devil's brew has he cooked up, Phantom?"

he groaned. "What does he mean — tonight will finish it?"

"I wish I knew," the Phantom said soberly. "But it's clear enough that we'd better be prepared. Yet if you throw too big a force around the station, you might scare them off. Steve and I will be there and ready for trouble. You can detail as many men as you can safely hide in the neighborhood. At least we know about what time they'll strike. But just the same I think Steve and I will get over there right away."

"Right," Mathers approved. "I'll get busy, too."

"One more thing," the Phantom said. "They dropped Jobe off in the two hundred block on Amity Street. Wilkin's car came out of the alley between numbers two hundred ten and two hundred and sixteen. Maybe Jobe ought to be picked up, if you can find him."

"I'll attend to that also," Mathers promised. "At least we've got plenty on Jobe. Phantom, maybe this time they'll walk into a trap."

The Phantom and Huston hurried out to where their car was parked and drove straight toward the TV station. They circled the block once. Everything seemed quiet. The Phantom parked the car just around the corner from the entrance.

"Get behind the wheel," he told Steve, "and keep your eyes on me. I'll be in that doorway directly opposite the entrance to the station. If anything happens, start moving fast."

Huston glanced at his watch. "We've got plenty of time, though, if Wilkins meant what he said about nine-thirty being the time he'd move in."

"He might work quicker than that, Steve. At this stage of the game we can't afford to take any chances. If I see something you don't, or can't see, I'll signal with my flashlight. Keep the motor running. . . . What about a gun?"

"I borrowed one from Sergeant Mathers." Huston patted his coat pocket. "I'm all set."

"See you later then."

The Phantom got out of the car. He crossed the intersection, slowed to a saunter and carefully studied the neighborhood. There were only a few people on the streets, and none of them acted suspiciously. None of the cars parked nearby were occupied.

The Phantom stepped into the doorway he selected, transferred an automatic from shoulder clip to coat pocket and kept a finger curled around the trigger. It was eight-thirty. An hour to wait if Wilkins had timed it correctly.

In a few moments, Sergeant Mathers' police guards should arrive. Even Wilkins, with all his ingenuity, was going to have a hard time pulling any sort of job here tonight. That was what the Phantom was thinking, but he didn't have much faith in his own thoughts.

Five minutes went by. Cars were moving up and down the street, people kept passing by. So far none of the detectives had showed up, but it would take a little time for Mathers to assemble them. This was not a great city where any number of men were on police duty at all hours.

Then the Phantom saw a shiny new gray sedan rolling along the street at a fairly good speed. It passed him and its brake lights flashed. The car began moving in toward the open parking space directly in front of the TV station.

The Phantom hadn't been able to see who was in it, but the car was not going to stop. It seemed the driver only meant to swerve in as close as he could get to the entrance and be prepared to get away on a burst of speed.

Blinking his flashlight toward Steve, the Phantom barged out of the doorway, running as fast as he could travel toward the car which was now only crawling.

Suddenly he saw an oblong package sail out of the car window and land just outside the door of the station. The car began to pull away. The Phantom leveled his gun and fired twice. He saw the rear window cobweb, but the escaping car only sped up.

Without slowing up, the Phantom kept at a dead run straight to where that package lay. He swept it up and kept on going, but he veered quickly and dropped the package in the middle of the road. That was the best he could do.

He yelled at Steve who swiftly maneuvered the car to block the road. He was fifty yards away from where the package lay. The Phantom ran in the opposite direction, signaling oncoming cars to stop.

Suddenly the package, lying so innocently in the middle of the road, exploded with a roar. Fire was thrown in all directions. Some blazing chemical formed rivulets of fire, but on the pavement the flames were harmless. A few cars parked nearby were spattered with the stuff but none of them caught fire.

The Phantom sprinted toward the car which Huston was already straightening out. Traffic had piled up behind him, police whistles were screeching, and sirens were beginning to moan in the distance. The road was covered with broken glass from windows shattered by the explosion, and flames seemed actually to be consuming the pavement.

Huston opened the car door, and the Phantom climbed in hurriedly

"Get going!" he ordered. "The left side of the road isn't flaming too much. Get through it. We've got a car to catch!"

Huston bumped the left wheels over the curbing, roared through the fire and veered back on the road when they were safely past the danger. They reached the corner where there was a gasoline station. Two attendants were on the sidewalk looking down toward the scene of the explosion.

"A gray sedan with a shattered rear window!" The Phantom called. "Which way?"

Both men pointed south. Huston saw the signal, turned the corner and stepped on it. Twice more they stopped to ask if the car had been seen. Apparently the driver was either frightened or he had been wounded by one of the Phantom's slugs. The car was weaving badly, according to the people who were asked.

CHAPTER XVIII

PILLAR OF FIRE

Only for one thing, it was an easy trail to follow. At first the car they were after kept so well ahead of them that they never caught sight of it until they were far out of town and streaking along a state highway. Then Huston spotted a tail-light which kept moving from one side of the road to the other.

As they drew closer to it the Phantom leaned far over, put his right arm out of the window and pointed his automatic at the back of the car. Huston was gaining on it steadily. When they were within range, the Phantom fired twice.

As if those slugs had hissed a warning that could not be denied, the driver ahead straightened out his car and stepped on the gas. There was no longer any weaving; just straight ahead and excellent driving.

"He's going to get away from us," Huston grumbled. "That's a heavier car than ours and that boy really knows how to handle it."

"He'll slow for the next corner," the Phantom said tightly. "He'll have to — but you keep your foot on the gas pedal. I've seen you handle a car before. Give it all you've got, Steve."

Huston gripped the wheel hard, intent on following the Phantom's orders. Ahead of them the escaping car did slow down. The driver touched the brakes, and as tires began to scream, Huston tramped heavily. He gained fifty yards in seconds.

Twice more the Phantom's gun flamed. He was aiming for tires or the gas tank, but not having much luck. The road was none too smooth and his own fairly light car jounced considerably.

Then Huston hit that curve. It took some expert driving to keep the wheels on the road. In fact, the Phantom would almost have been willing to swear that none of them clung to the pavement. But when Huston straightened the sedan out, they were close to their quarry. Again, the Phantom fired. Nothing happened, so he brought his arm closer to the car, supporting it against the window. He leaned out and took sighted aim.

"Steady!" he yelled to Huston. "Hold her steady for a second."

He fired three fast shots. The car ahead gave a wild lurch

and almost tipped over. It left the road, smashed through thick brush and kept on going over a rutted but fairly well-cleared field.

For a full minute or two, neither Huston nor the Phantom could see the car and Huston couldn't stop short. But he skillfully lessened his speed, put the car into reverse and backed up fast. They could see the tail-lights of the other car now, out in the field.

Huston shifted gears and headed for the car. But before he had a chance to stop, the Phantom tore the door open, leaped out and began running toward the swath cut through the brush. He was within a hundred feet of it when a vast column of fire suddenly enveloped the car. There was an explosion, more pronounced than the one back in town. It blew off the car doors and the fire spread like a flash of lightning.

At the first warning, the Phantom threw himself flat and stayed there until there was no longer any danger of falling debris. Then he approached as closely as he could. Through the flames he could see someone slumped over on the front seat.

Huston was at the Phantom's side by now. Both of them closed their eyes and turned away. Neither spoke for some moments after the flames began to die down.

Then Huston murmured in a thick voice: "Talk about a taste of your own medicine —"

"Walk beside me," the Phantom told him. "Keep the beam of your flash on the ground. We're looking for footprints. There's too much grass here to make hunting much good, but whoever else was in that car ran hard to get away before the explosion. Maybe he dug his heels in deeply enough to have left marks."

"Who ran away?" Huston gaped at him. "Do you mean there was more than one man in that car?"

The Phantom nodded emphatically. "I do," he said. "I put some slugs into the back of that car, but I didn't hit a tire. I gave that up as impossible and began aiming at the driver. But when the car left the road, it looked as if it had a flat. Somebody was trying to make us believe that."

"But why?" Huston asked.

"Whoever it was hoped we'd think only one man was in the car and that he died when one of those incendiary bombs went off. But, Steve, if I'd hit that bomb with a bullet, the car would have blown up instantly. I think that bomb was touched off after the driver had a chance to get away, during the time we were backing up and hurrying over here. In the darkness, he had an easy time of it. Throw your light about here. . . ."

Huston obeyed. The Phantom bent over, signaled to Huston to follow him with the beam. Finally he came to a stop and pointed. There was a faint trail of crushed grass leading to the brush.

"You were right," Huston said. "There was somebody else in that car. But why didn't he try to do something to save his pal?"

"Perhaps the man in the burned car wasn't a pal, Steve. I also believe now that the driver weaved the car badly so it would be noticed and we'd have a trail to follow."

"Yeah — maybe." Huston nodded. "But it's a cinch the man in that car right now will never be identified."

"I know who he is," the Phantom said. "Or at least I can make a pretty good guess. And from a police circular I saw about him, he has some distinctive dental work which can help prove I'm right in my identification."

"Jobe!" Huston breathed. "Hank Jobe, the bank cashier whose prints were found on that bottle!"

"I'm sure it's Jobe," the Phantom said.

"Well, anyway," Huston sighed, "you stopped them from burning out Woodward's television station. That was fast work, Phantom."

"Maybe, but spiced with plenty of good luck," the Phantom said. "We'll wait here. Sergeant Mathers ought to be along pretty soon and when that car cools off, we'll make certain that Jobe was inside."

Sergeant Mathers was prompt — and surprised. The moment the fire died down sufficiently he set to work on a brief, temporary investigation, but it was enough to prove the Phantom right.

Leaving some men at the scene of the tragedy, the sergeant rode back to town with the Phantom and Steve Huston.

"First Lang," he said solemnly, "then Finley, and now Jobe. The dental work back there checked perfectly. Phantom, what's it all about?"

"I think I'm beginning to understand just what," the Phantom said slowly. "But first we want to nail Wilkins if we can. What did you do about him, Sergeant?"

"As soon as I got the news about the explosion at the TV station I threw a cordon of men around his apartment house. If he was inside then, he's still there. Do you want to be in on the kill?"

"If there is one," the Phantom said. "Steve, head for that apartment house."

"Anyway," Mathers went on, "I rescued something out of all this. Remember the phone clicks as Wilkins dialed that number to tell somebody he was all set to finish off the station?"

"You traced the call?" the Phantom asked.

"We did — and there's no question about who Wilkins called. That was the number of Gordon Pulver's house phone."

"Does he know you traced the call, Sergeant?"

"No — but I sent some men out there, too. They reported over my car radio that Pulver was at home and they were going to keep him there,"

"But first," the Phantom said, "we'll see what's what with Mr. Wilkins."

When they got there they found the apartment house well-covered. With drawn guns, and backed up by a dozen men, Mathers, the Phantom and Steve Huston sent the elevator to the ninth floor, filed down the corridor toward the apartment which Wilkins rented under another name, and Mathers assigned his men to stations which would prevent any possibility of the man's escape.

The Phantom stepped up to the apartment door and pushed the buzzer. He waited a full minute before he bent down and studied the lock. Then from a secret pocket he removed his kit of miniature burglar tools, selected one, and slipped the thin instrument into the keyhole. He did not have to make a second try, for he had made a study of all varieties of locks, and this particular one was familiar to him. A few gentle probings and the instrument caught hold. He turned the bolt back.

Mathers twisted the knob, kicked the door wide and the men with him braced themselves. Nothing happened. All lights were on inside the apartment. They found plenty of evidence that several men had been here, but this trap didn't close on anyone. "They got clear before we could move in," Mathers groaned. "When are *we* going to get a break?"

The Phantom didn't reply. He went over to a living room window and opened it wide. Outside was a fire-escape. He crawled out on it, asked for a flashlight and began studying the steel structure. In a few moments he was back.

"Sergeant," he said, "that fire-escape is old and has been allowed to rust through in spots. One whole section has broken away. You'll probably find the pieces in the courtyard which happens to be cemented. If you'll take scrapings of cement and compare it with the cement particles lodged in the clothing of George Lang, the man found at the foot of the television tower, I think you'll find the samples match."

"You mean Lang was killed by a fall from this fire-escape?" Mathers asked.

"I'm pretty sure he was. I think Lang was held prisoner here. For some reason we'll soon find out, they dressed him in the clothing of a tramp, I imagine they intended to kill him anyway, but my guess is that Lang slipped out the window and nearly got away. But the fire-escape broke and he fell nine floors. So they simply picked him up, hurried him to the tower and carried his body up it for some distance before letting it fall on the rocks."

"I'll get the cement samples," Mathers promised. "And I'm also going to haul Pulver in. He's going to have to explain a lot of things, but mainly the phone call Wilkins made to him."

"Just a moment," the Phantom said. "Are your men still monitoring the phone tap?"

"Far as I know they are."

The Phantom said: "There are two phones in this apartment — one in the bedroom. I'm going to try an experiment. Stand by this phone. When I signal you, pick it up and start talking."

"Okay." Mathers moved toward the telephone. "Whatever you say, Phantom."

The Phantom entered the bedroom, lifted the phone in there from its cradle. He dialed rapidly, waited until he heard the automatic buzz, then signaled Mathers who picked up his phone.

"Sergeant," the Phantom said into the phone, "if Pulver claims he wasn't at home to receive the call Wilkins made, or that nobody was on the wire when he did answer, you can believe him. Because Wilkins could have dialed, broken the connection before Pulver could answer, and one of his men could have used the phone you're holding, pretended he was

Pulver answering from his home and have carried on a faked conversation. All for the benefit of your men who were listening in. They'd hardly guess it was a trick."

"Just the same," Mathers grunted, "I'm going to question Pulver about this."

"I think you should," the Phantom agreed. "It's time for a showdown anyway. Why not bring him to Headquarters? Have Brennan there, too — and Woodward. Let's get them all together."

"Meet me in my office in half an hour, Phantom," Mathers said. "They'll all be present."

CHAPTER XIX

MOTIVE FOR MURDER

Mathers kept his word. Shortly after all the men the Phantom had mentioned had been assembled in Police Headquarters, he faced the group. Pulver was highly nervous. Woodward seemed angry about the whole thing, and the attitude of Brennan, as usual, was one of defying them all.

"Tonight, Mr. Woodward," the Phantom said, "your television station was almost destroyed. The next time the vandals might not miss. We've got to know the answers to all this death and destruction, and quickly. I'm positive that Chester McLean could help us, but for some reason he's afraid to return. However, he must be made to come back at once."

"But how?" Woodward asked. "We haven't the slightest idea where he is."

"There's one way to reach him," the Phantom said. "Sergeant, if you'll make an appearance on Woodward's television during the news broadcast, perhaps you can tell McLean it's safe for him to come back. No matter where McLean is, he will be watching television. He's bound to be. This whole affair stems from television, and McLean does own half the station here."

Woodward headed for the door.

"The best idea yet!" he exclaimed. "It will certainly bring him back. Come with me, Sergeant, and I'll arrange the broadcast. We haven't much time before the news is on."

After they were gone, Pulver turned to the Phantom. Without waiting to be questioned, he blurted:

"Phantom, I'm being framed! Mathers told me about those crooks calling my phone number. Well, they did all right, and I answered the phone at exactly the time Mathers said the call was put through. But there was no one on the wire. I swear it!"

"All right," the Phantom said. "Nobody's accusing you. You're free to go any time you like."

Pulver started for the door. "Thanks. For a moment I thought I'd be locked up."

The Phantom went out into the corridor with Pulver and closed the door.

"I think you can feel safe now," he told the man. "When McLean returns, I'm sure he'll clear everything up. I'll call you when we hear from him."

Pulver offered his hand. "Thanks again, Phantom. Odd, but I had an idea you were hot on *my* trail. I must have been wrong. Please do call me. I'm tremendously interested."

The Phantom returned to the office. Brennan was apparently eager to get away, too. The Phantom sat down and regarded the ex-gangster for a moment.

"You know, Brennan," he said after a moment, "everything about this affair points straight at you. That's because of your record and your eagerness to force your way into this television business."

"I'm through with that," Brennan declared. "What do I want any more money for, anyway? And I'm through with this city, too! I've had enough."

"I wouldn't try to leave if I were you until after McLean returns," the Phantom advised. "Sergeant Mathers might object."

"Look!" Brennan said, "I got nothing to do with this whole business except for trying to bluff McLean and Woodward into letting me in. I want this straightened out before I go, and I'll wait until you tell me it's all clear."

"Right," the Phantom said. "I'll call you as soon as I hear from McLean."

Brennan stormed out of the office. Steve Huston lit a cigarette and looked up at the ceiling.

"Maybe I'm wrong," he said thoughtfully, "but you're treating those guys with kid gloves. Is it because you're baiting a trap and smearing the lure with honey?"

"It could be." The Phantom grinned. "Of one thing I'm certain — it won't be long now."

It was almost midnight when Sergeant Mathers returned, highly excited.

"It worked!" he gloated. "I wasn't off the air ten minutes before McLean phoned Woodward at the TV station. He's willing to return, especially after I told him Lisa was safe and nobody could get at her."

"Where was he?" the Phantom asked.

"Hiding out, not forty miles from here. He's leaving right away, in a rented car."

"Do you know which road he'll take to get here?" the

Phantom queried.

"There's only one. Route 47. I'd better go meet him on the outskirts, eh?"

"No," the Phantom said, "I'll meet him. I have a special reason, Sergeant. You can help by phoning Hugo Brennan and telling him McLean is coming back. But tell him it's by train. Say he'll be in on the twelve-forty."

"If you say so," Mathers agreed, with a puzzled expression.

"Then call Pulver and tell him McLean is flying back and expects to land around one in the morning."

"What's the gimmick?" Mathers asked. "Do you think they'll try anything?"

"If they do, we'll be ready for them," the Phantom promised. "All right, Steve, let's get started. We're going to travel fast."

Under the Phantom's direction, Steve Huston drove far out on Route 47. They came to a short section of highway which was under repair, making it necessary for any car to proceed slowly and cautiously over the rough surface.

"We'll wait here," the Phantom instructed. "We're far enough away from town now."

"You're going to stop McLean?" Huston asked.

"Yes, Steve. And we'll change cars with him. If a trap has been set, it will be sprung on us, and we'll be ready for it. McLean can double back to his hideout in our car, and wait until this blows over."

Huston suddenly sat bolt upright. "You're sure that McLean is going to be stopped and maybe knocked off? By Wilkins and his boys?"

"Yes — Wilkins," the Phantom said softly. "I want to meet him again, Steve. He's a ruthless sort when he has a man tied up. My face is still sore from the beating he gave me. And we want him for his part in these murders."

"Yeah, that's right," Huston said and added thoughtfully, "Now you had Sergeant Mathers tell Brennan that McLean was coming by train. Pulver thinks he's on his way by air. If a trap is set and sprung, it won't be by either of those two. But there's one other man who likely knows the truth — that McLean is driving back. And that man is Woodward."

"You're right, Steve." The Phantom nodded. "I've suspected him for quite some time."

"But why?" Huston asked. "What made him try to sabotage his own television station?"

"Steve," the Phantom said, "I don't believe Woodward owned that station at all. In fact, I'm almost willing to bet it was owned by four different people, three of whom are dead."

"I don't get it," Huston said with a puzzled frown. "And I don't mind admitting it."

"Look at the affair this way." The Phantom was watching the highway intently as he spoke. Now and then he studied an approaching car carefully. There was little traffic moving at this time of night. "You see, Steve, we have three dead men. In each case their identities were carefully concealed, or so the murderer hoped. Each of these three men came from widely separated parts of the country. It's hardly possible they had ever met. What's more, each of them must have had quite a lot of cash on hand — pretty hot money, if they tried to spend any great sum. Do you understand so far?"

"Yes — and maybe I'm a little ahead of you." Huston nodded. "But keep talking."

The Phantom nodded, and went on explaining.

"George Lang had been in the black market. His profits must have been in cash or he'd have been in trouble with the tax collectors. Finley was suspected of having robbed a bank. There was no real evidence against him, but if he suddenly began spending large sums, there would have been. The third man, Jobe, was an absconding bank teller who was well-heeled when he ran off. He might have spent some of the money, but apparently he didn't."

"Okay," Huston said. "We've got three men, heavy with dough, but the kind they couldn't spend. So what?"

"Now suppose a glib-tongued person came along and told these men how they could secretly invest a large part of their money. As part owner of an important television station, each could remain in the background, but draw his profits. If the station failed, though, they couldn't howl for their money back. Neither of them could afford to have it known he had that kind of money."

Huston closed his eyes and exhaled slowly. "Woodward sold a half interest in his TV station four different times," he muttered, amazed. "To men who had no comeback. Is that what you're driving at?"

"I can't prove it yet, but I'm certain I can tomorrow. Steve, Woodward came here without much cash. He managed to start a small, unimportant TV station which had little chance of amounting to much. Yet he could build up great promise for it if he had money enough to make it bigger. I know that George Lang brought some papers with him when he came here, and they looked like stock certificates. These were stolen from his hotel here in town. I also know one other thing. Lang made several phone calls to this city and in each case it was a person-to-person call — to Alonzo Woodward."

"Okay," Huston said. "If we take McLean's car and anybody stops us, we'll know it is Woodward."

"It will add to the proof," the Phantom said. "So we have Mr. Woodward with a small television station in which he has sold a large interest four times over. Then, unexpectedly, the coaxial cable is swung in this direction and the station becomes big and important. Worth a fortune."

"And those suckers thought they were rich! No wonder Woodward had them murdered. He did, didn't he?"

"Yes, I'm sure of it," the Phantom said. "There was so much profit involved now that none of the investors could take chances. Lang was the first to arrive. I suppose Woodward wanted to buy all of them out. He had systematically sabotaged his own station to such an extent that perhaps his investors would have accepted a reasonable offer. But much more than they'd put in — and they were obstinate. So Woodward hired his thugs and got busy."

"Wasn't Brennan in on it?" Huston asked.

"I doubt it. Brennan simply provided an excellent suspect. Perhaps he even gave Woodward the idea of how to try and work on his four partners to force them to sell their shares."

"Four partners!" Huston laughed. "Each owning a good part of the station. Brother — when it came time to pay off!"

"Woodward had to act before that time rolled around," the Phantom explained. "Lang refused to sell, so he was taken prisoner. Perhaps Woodward was going to force him to sign back his share. But that would have been dangerous, because Lang could have got Woodward into a lot of trouble if he ever heard about the other victims."

"So he had Lang murdered," Huston commented sadly.

"No, Steve. Woodward certainly intended to murder him, even had him dressed as a tramp to make identification harder, but Lang tried to escape and was killed accidentally . . . Hold it! This might be the car. It will have marked plates lettered 'Private Livery.' In this state, rented cars have special plates. That's how we'll know it's McLean."

But the car worried its way over the rough road without being stopped. It had regular marker plates. The Phantom went on with his story.

"So they had a corpse on their hands and didn't know what to do with it What with all the sabotage that was going on, they figured if it looked as if the dead man had fallen off the TV tower, he'd either be passed off as a tramp who for some strange reason tried to climb the tower, or that he had been trying to sabotage the tower. Either way, they were rid of a dangerous corpse which they doubted would ever be identified."

"But wait a minute," Huston objected.

"Finley was the second victim, but I thought he was working with the crooks."

"We have only Woodward's statement for that, Steve. That night when all those things happened to the TV programs, there had to be crooks planted in the station. Woodward could have planted them and told them exactly what to do. Ordinary thugs wouldn't have the vaguest idea of how to interfere with a TV program. It's a new medium; people don't know much about it. I think Finley was smuggled into the station. Woodward had his own men to hit him, Woodward, on the head, tie him up and put him in that supply closet for what he must have thought would be a perfect alibi. Then they simply tossed Finley down the elevator shaft."

"And Jobe was to have died in the role of a man who tried to burn down the TV station," Huston said. "Those guys didn't buy stock when they bought into that station. They bought death."

"That's right, Steve," the Phantom agreed. "And in each case Woodward did his best to conceal the identity of his victim."

"When did you first get wise?" Huston asked.

"Almost at once. I went to see Woodward twice. The first time, I was attacked before I reached my hotel room. But Woodward didn't know in what hotel I was staying, what room I was in or what name I was using. However, McLean did. I told him. When we meet McLean, I hope he'll tell us he phoned Woodward after I left and told him about me."

"And your second visit to Woodward made you suspicious?" Huston asked.

"Yes. He suggested strongly that I talk to Lisa McLean. Then he had Lisa lured to that old sanatorium, knowing well enough I'd follow her. There we were both trapped. I wondered at which of us that attack was aimed. Now I think our deaths were of equal importance to Woodward. McLean can also assure us about that."

"And only Woodward knew you were going to see Lisa," Huston commented.

"That's right. The men who had been sent to kill us called me by name without even seeing me. So they had been tipped off all right. Then, a few hours ago I deliberately let Woodward know we had Wilkins' telephone tapped. Woodward then arranged Jobe's death. Of course the fire bomb thrown from that car wasn't meant to destroy the TV station. Woodward knew we would be on guard. And the driver of the car purposely left a trail for us to follow so we could actually witness the car blowing up."

"And then Woodward warned Wilkins to get out of there fast," Huston said.

"Yes, Steve. But I think we'll meet Wilkins before the night is over and when we do ... Steve, there's McLean's car!"

CHAPTER XX

TWO CONFESSIONS

Running out to the torn-up road with Steve Huston, the Phantom called to McLean, who recognized him at once. McLean brought his car to a stop, and quickly the Phantom explained everything he knew. It seemed a relief to Chester McLean to be able to talk — at last.

"Yes," he said, as the Phantom paused. "I guessed Woodward was behind all the trouble at the station. But not until after I ran away and had time to think. Thank you for what you did for Lisa. I heard all about that over the radio — and could guess more."

"Why did you run away?" the Phantom asked. "I think I know, but I'd rather hear you tell it."

"Things were getting dangerous. That sabotage seemed to be aimed at getting rid of me. That's why I asked Frank Havens to enlist your help. But before you showed up, I saw a man snooping around the station and I followed him. Now, of course, I know he was simply tolling me to the tower. When I got there I saw Lisa hovering over a dead man. I didn't know what had happened, but I wanted to protect her in case anyone tried to involve her in any way. I knew she couldn't have had anything to do with that man's death — but would others believe that? I also knew that she would fear I *had* had something to do with it. She had come there in answer to a mysterious phone call, the whole idea being for her to see and suspect me. She didn't see me, so I lied to you when I got back home, and said I had been home since the late afternoon, asleep. Somehow I don't think you were fooled for one second."

"I wasn't," the Phantom said. "But that doesn't explain why you ran away."

"I thought they were going to strike at me through Lisa, because of another horrible idea I had. If I died, Lisa would inherit my interest in the station, then she would be the next victim. But if I vanished, and those killers couldn't get at me, there would be no reason to kill Lisa, with me still alive. Maybe it was crazy figuring, but that was how it came out in my mind."

"You probably saved your life," the Phantom told him.

"However, they did strike at Lisa, as you already know. She's safe now, though, since I smuggled her to a place the killers can't possible know about . . . Tell me something. After I left your house that first time, did you tell anyone I'd been there?"

"Yes," McLean replied. "I phoned Woodward, I had no suspicion of him then, and I thought he ought to know you were here, wanting to help us."

"That explains how Woodward's hired thugs knew where I was staying, and what room I was in," the Phantom said.

"I was so sure Brennan was behind all this trouble!" McLean sighed. "But now I realize that was hardly possible. The sabotaging was all done from inside the station, and Woodward would have been careful about the men he hired. I can see now that Woodward must have done most of the damage himself. Though I still can't figure out why."

"When Woodward first came to this city, he started this station on a shoestring, didn't he?" the Phantom asked.

"Yes," McLean admitted. "And he ran into financial trouble. He came to me for help, and he was a convincing salesman."

"He also convinced at least three other people to buy substantial shares," the Phantom said, coolly exploding his bombshell. "He must have sold the station a couple of times. It was nothing but a confidence racket with him."

"Say — wait!" McLean exclaimed. "I remember now! After I gave him my financial support, Woodward put more cash into the business himself. Quite a lot of it. I wondered where he got it."

"Now you know," the Phantom said. "And then the station suddenly became a most valuable piece of property. Woodward wouldn't get a dime out of it because he had oversold the business, and his three secret partners would demand their share and he couldn't meet their demands. So he had to kill them."

"What a glib customer Woodward is!" McLean sighed.

"I expect, Mr. McLean, that we'll find he's a professional, confident man. He was quick to take advantage of Brennan's trying to muscle in, and of Pulver's resentment at losing his chance to start a TV station. But he's finished now."

"Let's hurry back and clean this up," McLean suggested.

"Not quite so fast," the Phantom warned. "Woodward's men will be waiting for you. He must realize you've probably guessed part of the truth by now. They're all set to see that you don't get back."

"You mean — kill me?" McLean asked.

"Yes. But when they strike, they'll find Steve Huston and me in your car. You take ours, give us a thirty-minute start, then drive back where you came from until the way clear . . . Let's go, Steve, before Wilkins begins to wonder why his trap isn't working."

Five miles from the torn-up section of road there was a dark, twisting section of highway. Huston drove McLean's rented car while the Phantom crouched far down out of sight. Both guessed the attack would come at this point where a driver had to slow down.

Suddenly a car pulled out and blocked the road. Huston leaned on the brakes and managed to stop fifty feet from the car. The Phantom didn't move, but both his guns were ready.

"Here they come!" Huston said. "Wilkins and two of his men."

"When they get twenty feet away, slide down out of sight," the Phantom ordered.

Huston watched the trio approach. Wilkins hadn't drawn a gun, but his two companions held revolvers slanted down. They gradually drew away from Wilkins so that if there should be opposition, they wouldn't be bunched.

"Now!" Huston whispered.

The Phantom had already unlatched the door beside him. He pushed it open, jumped out, his two guns leveled. The thugs fired fast. Too fast — for the sudden appearance of this armed man startled them. The Phantom's guns blazed. One of the thugs dropped in his tracks. The other one wheeled around and started lumbering away. He took about a dozen steps before he came to a stop and folded up.

Wilkins stood with both hands stiff and away from his body. The Phantom walked toward him.

"All right, Wilkins," he said. "I'll wait until you get your gun out. But when this is over, one of us is going to be dead."

Wilkins raised a hand to his mouth and wiped his lips.

"I — I haven't got a chance against you," he whimpered. "I'm not committing suicide. Look, give me a break and I'll tell you everything you want to know. You've got to have my help. All I want is a break."

"Turn around," the Phantom snapped. "Reach high and keep your arms there. I had an idea you wouldn't fight. Steve —"

Huston hurried over from the car. At the Phantom's order he circled Wilkins, approached him from the front and quickly disarmed the man. Wilkins lowered his arms and his shoulders drooped. Huston propelled him to the car and pushed him into the back seat. The Phantom climbed in beside the man.

"All right, Steve," he said. "Drive to the TV station. I think Woodward will be there waiting to hear how his trap worked. We'll have the pleasure of telling him all about it."

When Huston shoved Wilkins into Woodward's office, the television station owner jumped to his feet. The Phantom's gun covered him.

"Sit down, Woodward," the Phantom ordered crisply. "We've got the man who has been responsible for all of your trouble. I can prove that this man Wilkins here guided the sabotage, killing and kidnapping which the opening of your station instigated."

"I — I'm glad it's all over."

"It's over except for the prosecution of this man, Mr. Woodward. You'll help us put him in the electric chair where he belongs. You'll do all in your power to convict him, won't you?"

"Yes — yes, of course," Woodward replied nervously.

"Like fun you will!" Wilkins suddenly shouted. "It's every man for himself now, and I'm not going to stay quiet while you go free and let me take the rap. I'm talking, too — and I've got plenty to say."

Woodward gulped. "I — don't understand. I never saw this man before."

"Woodward," the Phantom interrupted, "you're itching to go for a gun. If you think it will do you any good, go ahead. I'm waiting."

"But — but I had no such idea!" Woodward cried.

"I thought not," the Phantom said. "Get up. We're going to Police Headquarters and arrange to have the rest of Wilkins' boys rounded up. Then you'll be given a chance to confess, if you like. It won't make much difference, because we've got plenty on you. After that, someone will have to straighten out the financial situation connected with this TV station. That's a job I'm glad I won't have to do because it will probably be harder than running you down, Woodward."

Woodward got up slowly. "I killed no one," he said sullenly. "I didn't want murder done. But Wilkins got out of hand. He refused to listen to me, and —"

"That's a lie!" Wilkins shouted. "I took my orders from you."

"We can argue it out later," the Phantom said. "But I'm glad to see both of you are in a talking mood. Steve, keep a gun on Wilkins. I'll escort Mr. Woodward. . . ."

It was morning before Sergeant Mathers finished extracting confessions from his prisoners. All of the Phantom's theories and facts were backed up. Woodward had sold the television station twice over, strictly as a confidence game which backfired when the station became a heavy money-maker. Sergeant Mathers wiped his face after the last signature had been affixed to the confessions.

"Steve," he said to the red-headed *Clarion* reporter, "this is the biggest case ever to hit my town. I'm glad the Phantom was here to help because without him, I'm afraid I'd still be floundering around trying to pin the blame on Brennan or Pulver."

"You wouldn't have been alone in that," Huston said, and grinned. "My money was on Brennan."

Mathers looked around. "I haven't seen the Phantom for a while. I'd like to thank him for —"

"He left some time ago," Huston said. "And he doesn't want any thanks."

"But at least you can tell him how much I appreciate —"

"Not me," Huston smiled. "I don't even know who he is."

"There must be some way," Mathers began.

"Forget it," Huston advised. "He'll have all the satisfaction he wants out of Woodward's conviction. And you'll hear of him again pretty soon, Sergeant. Somebody is going to think he has the world's best idea for getting rich quick without getting caught at it. Then you'll find the Phantom there, pitching straight balls. He doesn't go for the curves, Sergeant. He doesn't have to. Me, I'll go back to my job pounding out some crime stories for the *Clarion*, and keep hoping that before long the Phantom will need me."

THE END

A Full Book-Length Novel

THE VIDEO VICTIMS

BY ROBERT WALLACE

Taken from the Case-book of Richard Curtis Van Loan
(Profusely Illustrated)

A television myster novel featuring the Phantom!

Published by
Wildside Press, LLC
www.wildsidepress.com

Milestones of Murder originally appeared in Volume LVI,
Number 1, the Spring, 1951 issue of
The Phantom Detective magazine,
copyright 1951 by Standard Magazines, Inc.

THE PHANTOM DETECTIVE, by Robert Wallace!

The Dancing Doll Murders
The Black Ball of Death
Notes of Doom
Harvest of Death
Tycoon of Crime
Stones of Satan
Fangs of Murder

THE PHANTOM DETECTIVE, by Robert Reginald

The Phantom's Phantom
The Nasty Gnomes

PULP MAGAZINE FACSIMILES

The Black Mask Magazine, No. 2 (May 1920)
Ghost Stories (June 1931)
The Phantom Detective #1 (February 1933)
Sinister Stories (February 1940)
Spicy Mystery Stories (August 1935)
Spicy Mystery Stories (February 1937)
Strange Tales #7 (January 1933)
Submarine Stories (March 1930)
Tales of Magic and Mystery (February 1928)
The Thrill Book, (Sept. 1, 1919)
Weird Trails (April 1933)

THE MYSTERIOUS WU FANG

The Case of the Suicide Tomb, by Robert J. Hogan

OPERATOR #5

The Army of the Dead, by Curtis Steele
Blood Reign of the Dictator, by Curtis Steele
The Dawn That Shook the World, by Curtis Steele
Invasion of the Crimson Death Cult, by Curtis Steele
Liberty's Suicide Legions, by Curtis Steele
Revolt of the Devil Men, by Curtis Steele
Winged Hordes of the Yellow Vulture, by Curtis Steele

SECRET AGENT ôXö

The Assassins League, by Brant House
Claws of the Corpse Cult, by Brant House
The Hooded Hordes, by Brant House